NOWHERE FAST

Published by ECW Press
2120 Queen Street East, Suite 200, Toronto, Ontario, Canada M4E 1E2

NATIONAL LIBRARY OF CANADA CATALOGUING IN PUBLICATION

Blake, Yashin
Nowhere fast / Yashin Blake

ISBN 1-55022-645-2

1. Title

PS8553.L3436N69 2003   C813'.6   C2003-907289-4

Editing: Michael Holmes / a misFit book
Cover and Text Design: Darren Holmes
Production and Typesetting: Mary Bowness
Printing: Marc Veilleux

This book is set in Bembo.

The publication of *Nowhere Fast* has been generously supported by the Canada
Council, the Ontario Arts Council, the Government of Canada through the Book
Publishing Industry Development Program. Canada

DISTRIBUTION
CANADA: Jaguar Book Group, 100 Armstrong Avenue, Georgetown, ON, L7G 5S4
UNITED STATES: Independent Publishers Group, 814 North Franklin Street,
Chicago, Illinois 60610

PRINTED AND BOUND IN CANADA

ECW PRESS
ecwpress.com

NOWHERE FAST

Yashin Blake

MISFIT

ECW PRESS

CONTENTS

These stories are for the Blakes:
Mira, George, and Arun.

ANOTHER MOZART

"McCoy Tyner. McCoy Tyner. Ach. Who even knows who this McCoy Tyner is?" Old Schmidt had had a most unsatisfactory piano lesson. Actually, it was most satisfactory. Sublime even.

"Tyner was Trane's pianist, from the classic quartet." The guy in line behind Schmidt had turned down the volume on his headphones to answer Schmidt.

"What?" Schmidt exclaimed once he realized who had spoken. He'd always assumed that young people with headphones could hear nothing but *boompf, boompf, boompf.* Completely cut off from humanity they are, which is what they preferred.

"You said Tyner, right? McCoy Tyner." It suddenly occurred to the young man, whose name was Jason, that the old coot could be nuts. That maybe the name he was muttering was a coincidence.

"He's a pianist, ja?"

"Ja, I mean yes," Jason said. He stopped there, even though the old man was looking at him expectantly — they'd reached the front of the line. Jason could sense the people behind him stretching out diagonally so they could read the coffee of the day chalkboard and see how picked over the muffin and danish display was. They could also watch everybody else order their drinks, fumble with change, get confused over the names of the various sizes, the fat free, the lactose free, the with cinnamon or without questions.

"Can I help who's next please?" A pierced latte slinger

said impatiently. Schmidt started and turned. "Ah," he looked at the price board for a moment, trying to remember where he was. "Espresso, espresso," he said.

The barrista rang up a double. Schmidt didn't notice when he was handed his change, but brightened when he saw the size of his beverage. Jason gave him a wide berth, despite his curiosity.

"You were asking about McCoy Tyner?" A woman in her mid-thirties sat down across from Schmidt and put an old leather folio down on the table.

"You are a musician?"

"French horn."

"Where did you study?"

"Here. Alberta. Holland for three months."

"Who was your teacher in Banff?" Schmidt continued his inquest.

"Farber. Eliot briefly, then Jorgenson."

"You made it into Jorgenson's class, eh?" Schmidt raised an eyebrow and sipped espresso.

"My friend pointed you out to me as I came in. Says you don't know who McCoy Tyner is."

"Ach, again with this Tyner fellow." Schmidt was offended by the name.

The horn player's name was Lara. She scanned the packed coffee bar. If she hadn't started talking to Schmidt she would have taken her chocolate croissant and latte to the park bench down the street. But she had her period and the thought of walking, not to mention sitting in the cold, to get a caffeine and chocolate fix brought her down. "He used to play in John Coltrane's quartet. Back in the mid-sixties," Lara tried. "He's a jazz pianist."

"I am a pianist, Leopold Schmidt," he said. Take that.

"I see," Lara for some reason said. She realized she

hadn't bit into her croissant yet and did so at once, hoping to hit the chocolatey stuff right away. She took a big hit of latte and let the hot, creamy unsweetened liquid melt into the pastry in her mouth. The heroin-like effect took her mind away from her aching uterus. She almost forgot the cranky old man.

"This Tyner, tell me more."

"He's still alive. He comes through town every couple of years, with a trio or his big band."

"Is he good? As a musician, I mean. You are a musician. A well-trained professional musician even though you play only the French horn. Tell me, musician to musician. Can he really play?"

Just what she needed, another superior-minded pianist. Lara paused, then leaned across the table to give her words more significance. "He's very good."

"I see, I see." Schmidt seemed to ingest the drama. It left him at a loss.

"He played at our wedding."

"We played him at our wedding." The correction came from the male half of a couple sitting at the next table. They were drinking out of mugs and had taken their coats off, unlike Schmidt and Lara.

"We couldn't help overhearing. We played 'A Love Supreme' at our wedding ceremony. The Coltrane recording, of course. But Tyner's an integral part of it." The man's name was Hugh. He and Meredith had been married seven years previously, in the field behind the grade school they'd both attended. The photos had been tricky, since the school was, by then, boarded up. Vandals burned it down eight days later.

"Everybody seems to know this musician but me. Tell me, does anybody listen to the classics anymore? Music that wasn't composed last week. Mozart. Haydn. Pianists?" Schmidt's last word was accompanied by a flamenco dancer's twisting wave of the hand. "Do any of you even know one classic? *The Tempest* for example?"

"*The Tempest*. I know that but I really prefer the histories. *Henry V*," Hugh said.

Lara started to laugh.

"The St. Crispin's Day speech," Meredith encouraged.

Schmidt was confused.

"We few, we happy few, we band of brothers." The couple were amateur actors; they'd joined a neighbourhood theatre to revive their marriage four years ago and it had worked beautifully.

"No, no, no," Schmidt said, banging his fist on the table. "Beethoven, *Piano Sonata 21, Opus 32*. Music. Not words." Other customers stared and the manager stood on tiptoes, peering over the cappuccino machine to see what the commotion was. A friendly discussion he decided quickly, seeing the length of the lineup, and looked back down only to realize he'd totally forgotten if he was making a caf or decaf, fat or nonfat.

"Beethoven," the actor repeated to appease the old man.

"Why the interest in McCoy Tyner anyhow?" asked Lara, annoyed.

"I am piano teacher. Retired. But I still have a few students. I go to people's homes and teach their children. I don't charge much. I feel I did not spend enough time with my own — but that's another matter.

"A new student I have. Five years old. Brilliant. Stunning. A perfect ear. Her dexterity on the keyboard is innate. A gift of God, without a doubt. And it has taken me six months to decide. To admit that what I saw, what I *heard* and felt the first time I met her is true. I haven't said a word. Just taught and watched and listened. Today I had her perform for her parents. Her father and his girl-friend really. I said, 'Listen!' And they did. When she finished the father looked surprised. He said, 'So she plays notes written on paper?' I said, 'Yes, beautifully,' and wanted to explain further. But he interrupts. This father is very rude. He asks, 'Can she improvise yet?' and starts laughing like the whole thing is a joke.

"Improvise? Play what isn't even there? Why? She can play magic already. Five years old. *The Tempest. The Mirror Sonata. The Sled.* And he laughs some more and says she doesn't sound like McCoy Tyner. That's it. McCoy Tyner. To him this is a pianist."

"He is good," Lara said again, but hopefully in a way not to offend Schmidt.

"It sounds like he hired the wrong teacher." Hugh said, instantly raising his hand to pacify the old timer. "I mean, if he likes jazz piano and doesn't know or like the classics . . ." he shrugged sympathetically.

"Please," the old man said. "I know what I am talking about. I played with the Wiesbaden Symphony for years. I performed all over Europe with chamber groups. Solo. Then I came to this country. I taught at the conservatory. At the university. And still I performed. Now I am retired. I teach children for little money because I love it. And please," he begged these strangers in the coffee shop, "I know. This child is a genius."

It was that simple.

Lara was slumped low in her chair now. Crumbs on the empty pastry wrapper on the table, latte vacuumed down. She felt like taking a bath. Or going to sleep. As it was she'd be late for work. She was going to use the photo-copier there to copy the scores in her folio. A friend had written them. A film student's soundtrack. She thought about geniuses. History books were full of these sort of people. She'd met two in her life. Musical geniuses. Their lives hadn't played out in any heroic way. For one of them it was oceans of beer and farmyard after farmyard of pot and one obscure, eccentric local band after another. For the other it was mommy's basement, per-manently unwashed hair, stray bottles of expired meds, and boxes and boxes of scores and homemade recordings he was much too paranoid to let anyone hear.

She wasn't impressed. It was an ugly and depressing affair.

"How old is this kid, again?" Meredith asked.

"Five."

"What do you think they should do? I mean five — the kid isn't even in grade one."

"Grade one. This child is already a graduate of grade seventeen, eighteen. I don't care what you say. Let the child perform. Let the world hear her music, see her tal-ent. The record companies will come and the composers will come with special music written for this child to realize." Schmidt was expansive.

"But the spotlight so early . . ." Hugh said.

"The child will be destroyed," Lara said. "A freak. Never normal. Playing. Discovering things at a natural pace."

"The price of the gift."

"A high price," Meredith said.

"Not to do it for the money. Not for the parents or the record companies. For the world to see what God can create. It is a miracle. For the music. How many normal childhoods are there already? Let normalcy be destroyed in this one case."

Hugh opened his mouth to agree, but Lara spoke first. "It's not worth it," she said, standing, picking up the folio of soundtrack music. "Genius isn't necessarily a blessing. And buy yourself a McCoy Tyner record — you might learn a thing or two."

Lara held onto the back of her chair for a moment as a cramp jabbed through the bottom of her body. She tilted forward slightly and her breathing became tight. It ruined the drama of her exit, but the spasm subsided and she turned and left.

WESTERN CREAMERY

"When I was in high school I used to draw Jesus on the cross all the time."

"Really?"

"Yeah, I mean *all* the time. My big art project in my last year was this mural on one of the walls in the gymnasium. It featured Jesus up there with, y'know, oblivious skateboarders racing by in the foreground and the space shuttle up in the sky above." Sabby still got excited. It was only a couple of years ago.

"Cool." Dana meant what he said. He just didn't know if Sabby was a real Christian chick or if her school was some sort of hotbed of modern art.

They were about to watch *Fight Club*. An enormous popcorn balanced between them. They both ate quickly and ignored the one or two or three popped kernels that got lost between bag, hand, and teeth.

Sabby had little nub tits that punched cartoon bumps in her fuzzy sweater.

"I first drew Jesus on the cross when I was like, twelve or thirteen, and it was weird. It was like, I was so empowered by creating that. I mean, here it is, the most profound moment in our history and I could draw it up, a fifteen-second doodle or a fifteen day hour week airbrushed masterpiece. Only I never learned how to airbrush. My old boyfriend said I could do Jesus on the side of his van and I was going to learn but —" Sabby shrugged and hit herself in the mouth with a popcorn fist.

Dana stopped chewing. Why hadn't she learned? And who the fuck was this boyfriend, what happened with him? Why be jealous of a guy who's out of the picture? And what about Jesus on the cross?

The movie started.

One of Dana's boys was a few aisles back. Jean-Paul, looking stylish with yellow tints up on his head. He and Dana made a show of greeting one another, hand shaking, grinning, and assuring each other that things were "cool," that "not much" was going on.

Sabby and Jean-Paul's girl, Velda, checked out each other's eyebrows and nail jobs, compared their men for who they were, who they thought they were. They held each other's eyes. Then Dana led the way up the rest of the aisle and out while Jean-Paul and Velda listened to the last song, pretending to watch the rest of the credits through all the people now standing in front of them, coating themselves while talking loudly about the star of the movie and his famous girlfriend as if they were personal friends.

Dana and Sabby went to an expensive cocktail lounge that had a narrow upholstered bench down one wall with little round tables precisely twelve inches apart from one another. Dana took the simple wooden chair facing the table.

Partway through their second trick martini Dana left the chair and squeezed onto the bench beside Sabby and put his hand up her skirt. She let him stay, arresting his hand before it reached her sweaty panties — but only after he reached the bare thigh above her stocking. She almost fell on the floor at the little boy glee on Dana's face: the garter strap connecting his pornographic imagination to her elastic reality.

"Do you have a skateboard?" she asked.

"Motorcycle."

"Can I paint Jesus on the cross on the gas tank?"

"Sure. Why'd you stop anyhow? What happened?"

"I don't know, man. High school ended."

Dana knew that feeling. He removed his hand, filled it with his glass and took down a large swallow. Suddenly moody and philosophic. Suddenly less interested in being on this date. She sensed this shift. Leaned her face closer to his profile, opening her mouth to bring the moment back, immediately wishing she'd stayed still and just let it go. Like when her sister talked about life, her sister knew how to talk through scenes like this.

"Gotta whiz," Dana said and went downstairs.

Sabby, lost for a moment, adjusted the little 1940s big band jacket with the padded shoulders she had on over the sweater. Wondered about her makeup. Adjusted to being in *this* place, at *this* table, alone for a moment, exposed. Not at home on her couch with a bag of Cool Ranch Doritos babysitting her sister's kid. She checked out the other people out on a Saturday night. The blue martini had gone warm, coated her mouth and tasted like funk on the way down but she didn't mind. *Fuck it. I gotta pee too. Let him come back and wonder where —*

Sabby got up and defensively scanned for curious eyes: no one else in the place even knew Sabby existed.

Halfway down the stairs she saw Dana's back, he was talking on the pay phone. He didn't see her turn around and go back up.

He caught up with her signing the credit card thing, she hadn't had the twenty and the ten to make a smooth Hollywood exit.

"You got the bill. Good." He pointed at the document; the tip and total penned in by her Jesus hand. "I'll get you back for that." He was looking out the huge window at the city blowing down the street. She felt the need for him again now that he was back. Funny, in that moment of getting and settling the bill she thought she'd gotten over him.

On the sidewalk, a few doors down in the half light of a streetlight, they stopped. "I have a flask of Irish whiskey in my purse," she said. Drinking buddy. He was unbuttoning his shirt really fast, like it was on fire but he didn't want to wreck the buttons. He wasn't wearing a tie but he had on one of those hip, cheaply made suits that rich brats wore as pajamas.

"I lied. I do have a skateboard. Only —"

"No motorcycle?"

"Not yet. It's in a friend's shed right now. Norton Commando. He promised he'd sell it to me. Doesn't run though."

"No, eh?"

"No," Dana said and opened what he could of the shirt. The very top button was still done up.

"Jesus Christ."

"Yeah," Dana said.

Tattooed. Just the face, a close up of the cross scene, grossly disfigured with pain. Recognizable by the crown and the hippie beard.

"Nice."

"Thanks," Dana said.

The ice had actually broken when Dana got serious

about his drink and had to go downstairs.

"So."

"So."

"Look, why don't we just go in here and have a couple of drinks."

"Yeah. Okay."

They settled at the next table, this place less chi chi, less tony. This server had an exposed navel piercing instead of a white, starched shirt.

"Beer," Dana said. "Doesn't matter what kind." He was buttoning his shirt back up.

"Vodka and cran, in a pint glass, extra ice please."

Sabby took off the jacket she knew she paid way too much for — she was just so in love with the powder blue — pointing her tits at Dana as she did. She pulled a stray coaster napkin towards her and took out a pen. Before she could begin to draw, Dana said, "So are you a total Christian girl or what?"

"I was about to ask you the same thing."

My Sister

I met a thousand soldiers in Vietnam nicknamed Motown.
— Michael Herr, *Dispatches*

The Baker's house was on a wide street with enormous trees and long driveways. Garages were separate structures, set beside and slightly behind the big white houses. Neighbour's kids played on the tire swing that still hung from the big maple out front.

Mary Baker stood at the back screen door of her parents' house, looking out over the porch into the backyard. Butterflies flitted about her mother's perennial garden. Her father's rosebushes stood in a proud scraggle, the thorny arms authoritative and correct. It was very warm. All the windows were open, and a breeze circulating through the house from the front pushed her dress around her knees. Encouraging her to come outside and relax. Summer dress.

Mary thought about yesterday in the city. A carload of Negroes had been stopped by the police. All the occupants were made to get out. Something hadn't seemed right. But they must have done something wrong, otherwise the police wouldn't have stopped them.

Behind her, her mother took a pie out of the oven. Set it to cool. Only Ma Baker baked in the heat of the day. "Baker by name," she joked. Mary hated kneading and creaming and folding in but her mom had drilled the skills into her.

Mary pushed a wisp of hair off her forehead. She'd

finished high school at the beginning of summer and, against her parent's wishes, was going to college in the fall. College was for Mark. Mary would get married. Mark had gone all right, but dropped out after only a year, knowing that he was exposing himself to the draft. Mary thought Mark was vaguely anti-war but he'd answered the notice, actually volunteered for the Marines. Dad's old service. She knew Dad doubted this war. Mark's last meal with them, after boot camp and sniper school, before he shipped out, was eaten in total silence.

Mary had always wanted to go to university. She said she wanted a real education. She wanted to be able to make choices in life. That morning she and her father had gone to the bank to discuss a small loan to help with tuition. Mary knew there was still money in Mark's college fund and when he came home he'd have his GI Bill. But her father wanted it to seem like a burden, educating his daughter beyond secondary school.

The bank teller had been in Mary's class. He'd graduated too and was moving to the Midwest in the fall to study history.

"You certainly look pretty today, Mary," he told her. She smiled at him neutrally. Her father wanted more to happen here. Mary stayed away from boys. This teller, with his wispy mustache, posed too much of a threat to choices she didn't even know about yet.

A car pulled into the driveway and honked. Mother went out and joined Mrs. Ellis. The ladies were going for their weekly hair appointment. "Goodbye Mother," Mary called. Father was back at the office. Mary was feeling lazy. She put some coffee on to perk. She loved caffeine in the afternoons. She'd run around and clean all the second floor windows or read Henry James on the porch swing or lay in the tub and masturbate.

There was a noise in the front hall. Soft footsteps or mumbled voices. Mary couldn't be sure so she went to check. She was barefoot.

It was Mark. He was incredibly quiet. His face was gaunt but somehow he looked much bigger. Even bigger than after basic training. And wilder. He was a wild animal. Scared and hesitant but ready for violence.

He'd just walked in from a combat patrol in the jungles of outside Quang Tri, I Corps Vietnam. A black plastic rifle was in his hands. Another soldier came in behind him, closing the door. An enormous gun was cradled in his arms. Belts of golden bullets criss-crossed his chest and a shotgun, like dad's turkey gun only much, much shorter, hung from one shoulder as if an afterthought. They both wore muddy boots, half canvas, half leather. Hand grenades were clipped all over his torso. He had on a suit of armour. A pack hung awkwardly off his back and a helmet was tilted forward on his head, covering his eyebrows, making him look like a robot. Or a store mannequin. His body kept pulsating — sort of relaxing, then going stiff and quiet, like he was pretending not to be there. Invisible.

"Hello Mary," he said. It was Mark but it didn't look or sound like him. He looked right through her. Like she was already dead. Who else could it be? But why was he here? He hadn't called. Didn't they even get to shower and change before they came home? Or turn in their guns?

"Hello Mark."

He didn't answer for a long time. He turned stiffly from the waist, indicating his friend. "This is Motown. My bro. Saved my life," Mark explained. Mark held his weapon like he was on guard duty. Like trouble might come from the living room, or from behind Mary. Trouble from the kitchen. Death riding in on the smells of coffee and pie. A neat trick: death was like that. Mary could picture Mark firing a burst down the hall, hitting the ground, rolling, flipping a grenade into the living room. Motown would cover the stairs. Mary knew that. This is what her brother did now. Her brother who sat at the dinner table demanding to know the relevance of *Moby Dick* while the six o'clock news showed bodies being thrown onto the floor of a helicopter, then body bags in an anonymous row, then silver coffins being fork-lifted off a plane. With this final movement, the coffins were being saluted by a bunch of gleaming, nameless soldiers under an American sun.

Mary shifted her weight. She felt naked in her summer dress. Her mother had insisted she wear stockings to the bank despite the heat. The tense lines of the garter belt on her skin had irritated her and she'd changed as soon as she got home, but now she looked at, *felt*, the narrow, straining straps digging into Mark's and Motown's shoulders, down their chests to the heavy equipment belts resting on their hips.

"I'm glad you're home Mark. Mom and Dad are out but I know they'll be glad, too." Mary didn't know why she felt like she was lying.

Mark walked into the living room, looking around like he'd never been there before. Stray clumps of mud outlined each footprint he left in the deep carpet. Then, as if remembering where things were kept, he went through the wide arched doorway into the dining room, straight to the credenza. Half a dozen liquor bottles stood on a silver tray. An anniversary present. An empty ice bucket. A few crystal tumblers, inviting, if it weren't for the dust.

"Would you like a drink?"

But Mark had already picked up a bottle. The closest to him. He unscrewed the cap and dropped it, disassociating himself from it, as if the earth itself would open up and swallow it — like a grenade pin. He actually stepped on it as he adjusted his balance, preparing for what he seemed to anticipate as a moment of prayer and redemption. The cap pressed silently into the deep carpet.

For a moment, Mary felt as if she were suffocating. Mark drank. A third of the bottle. A smaller portion ran down his chin and glistened, dripping onto his fatigue shirt where it disappeared, dazzlingly, amongst the filth and stains he was already wearing.

"The thing is, Mary," he began, holding the bottle out to Motown. Motown silently unstrapped his machine gun, standing it in the corner, butt on the floor, golden belt of bullets pooling carefully around it. He took the bottle.

Motown drank with the same voluminous passion Mark did. Handed the bottle back. Mark drained it, eight or nine ounces of hard liquor in one long, refreshing swallow. Resurrection.

"The thing is Mary. Motown saved my life and —"

The doorbell rang. Mary turned quickly and opened it.

The bank teller, Richard was there. "Oh, hello Mary. Your father told me you might be in. You see, I have forty-five minutes to eat lunch and I was wondering if you'd like to walk to the park with me and —"

"Hey dirt bag!"

Richard hadn't seen Mark. He was so taken by the glow Mary had around her. And even now, looking at

Mark, he certainly didn't recognize him even though they'd played football together, less than a year ago, in the very park he'd just mentioned. The bank teller was distracted, not by Mark's appearance but by the grenade he was unhooking from his flak jacket. The pin he was pulling. The slow motion spoon flying off. The faint faint sizzle. The teller didn't know much about grenades but he knew that now it was only a matter of counting seconds.

"Get the fuck away from my sister, college boy!" Mark spoke with telepathic authority, keeping track of every single second. He was a good soldier. He'd just spent a little too long in the bush. Mark slammed the grenade into the bank teller's chest and with the same motion, shoved him out the door.

Mark slammed the one hundred-year-old oak door. The explosion on the other side shattered the two narrow floor-to-ceiling windows that flanked it.

"I promised Motown my sister for saving my fucking life." Mark said to the door, as if he could explain things to the dead.

Mary wanted to scream — wishing time back, and Mark's death, ten thousand miles away; but Motown's tongue came into her mouth like gooks through a breech in the wire, his lips mashing hers against her teeth. Wounded with your own weapon, on your knees in the mud, about to vomit from the pain, but briefly, strangely distracted by the reflection of some clouds in a puddle.

Motown pulled her against the bulky flak jacket that was an extension of his body and held her there for a moment, panting. Then he hefted her over one shoulder and started up the stairs. Mary was fixing to scream, but felt only darkness, closing off the light until there were only stars. No, spots, not stars. Just spots of light. She fainted.

Mark went and got another bottle, then used the muzzle of his rifle to nudge back an inch of his mom's lace drapery. Eventually, a police car pulled up out front. He looked dreamily over the front sight as an old chum's father got out, visibly shocked and repulsed by the smouldering remains of the bank teller. He pushed his cop hat to the back of his head.

Now, golly gee. I wonder what could have happened here. Mark pictured the thought bubble over the cop's head as he clicked the rifle from safe to rock and roll.

BY THE NUMBERS

7:10

"Oh," Lucielle said, opening her bedroom door. "I thought you'd come." She stood back and Max came in. They stood like that for a minute. Max was in a turtleneck and he seemed bigger than he was before.

Lucielle's parents' New Year's Eve party was already noisily gearing up. The Hanson's had arrived a few minutes ago and the Lieu's, from next door, had been over for dinner.

She wasn't sure what she'd do — join them, take a long walk, go to the meeting. She had no invitations, at least none that she'd acknowledged. Her self-imposed exile had been difficult to maintain at first, but by now it was hard to break. Lana, her maid of honour, hadn't even called.

But here was Max.

"I was on my way to Dale's place. Elvin's hosting a party there," he said, looking at her.

"When did you get out?" she asked.

"Earlier this month." He refused to let on that he'd convinced a naïve part of himself that she'd never visited because she didn't know he was inside. But, of course, it's a small world and jail time in their circle was reasonably big news. Up there with getting a scholarship or having an affair.

"Oh," Lucielle said again, and went back to her chair. It was her desk chair but she'd moved it over to the window. A yellowed bedspread, pilled and unravelling at the corner, was draped over it. Lucielle sat, pulled her knees up, and, with a long perfected motion, wrapped the comforter around herself. She looked outside into the incredibly dark backyard. Max may as well have not been there.

When they were teenagers, an hour could pass without either of them speaking. Listening to records. Doing homework. Making out. So Max flopped on his stomach across the bed, put his chin in his hands and bent his knees, letting his feet float in the air.

Lucielle looked over with a cordial smile she couldn't sustain. "So. What are you doing here?" She gave up on the smile.

"I thought we should talk," Max said, not really believing himself.

"Did you come here to fuck? A make-up fuck? A mercy fuck? A muckity muck fuck?"

Max rolled slightly onto one side for a moment and dug a cell phone out of his pocket. He tried to decide if this was an invitation or an expression of pain. "Lucy, Lucy, Lucy."

"What?" she said, sulkily, to the darkness beyond the window. "I haven't had sex since May."

Max stifled a grin.

"It's not funny!" Her lips fought their way out of a smile. "When did you have sex last?"

"Boxing Day." Max said matter-of-factly. "And before that Christmas Day and before that Christmas Eve."

"So you've come to rub my nose in it?" Lucielle asked.

Max got off the bed. He folded his arms and leaned against the faded wallpaper over by the closet.

"Well, I guess you had some catching up to do. I'm doing a sort of monk thing I guess. Hey, who you been having all that sex with?"

"A good Samaritan," Max said. Then smiled. "A good fucken Samaritan."

"A good fucken Samaritan with a tight pussy, huh?"

Max didn't remember Lucy being this vulgar, this bitter.

"You missed my wedding." Lucy said.

Max and Lucy had hooked up in the tenth grade. Gone out off and on through high school then grew closer once graduation spat them out into the world. When they were dating during school Max spent a lot of time at Lucy's house. He even helped her dad rebrick the chimney one Fall when the mortar had worn out and the bricks were simply stacked, waiting for one big wind to blow them down.

Max had always assumed he and Lucy would marry. He never pictured their wedding day, or imagined the honeymoon — it was more like assuming there'd be a Christmas next year. It would just happen. They had ups and downs. Ons and offs. But during one of the offs Lucy got herself engaged to some guy named Dan.

"I don't think I could have come."

"You mean even if you weren't in jail?"

"Yeah. Come on, watching you take the plunge with some other guy — after I screwed up what we had. That was painful enough."

"Painful for *you*?"

When Lucy found out that Max had slept with someone else during what had been a very long and fun "on" period, she slid into a three-day bender she couldn't remember. "I thought it fitting actually. You not being there to watch me get married was okay because you were under lock and key."

Max felt he didn't deserve that. Sorting things out with your people on the street was one thing. Being locked up was another. He used to trust Lucielle. Before he realized the irreplaceable value of trust. Before he looked around a range, at other men in orange coveralls, and wondered, with horror, about who could really be trusted. At first Max didn't say anything in his defence. And then: "I would have come to your side. We were good close friends once, and nobody should be humiliated like that."

"Left at the altar in a seven hundred dollar dress. I couldn't even cry; I was so shocked. And he was nowhere in sight. At least if he'd been there I could have laid into him."

"Fists of love, huh?"

"Damn straight." Lucielle hugged herself and rocked a little. "I like to think I held my chin up and walked back down the aisle with some kind of dignity. I mean, Lana was crying, but I wasn't. I think I dropped the bouquet, left it at the preacher's feet. Dan's best man was standing there, too. Shit, I think *he* was ready to marry me; he felt so bad. Plus, I know he thinks I'm cute. Mom tells me it's all on video somewhere."

"Jeez Lucielle." Max paced as best he could, tossing the little phone from hand to hand absently. He ended up by the window. A motion sensitive light suddenly illuminated the neighbour's yard. Nobody there.

"I would have come — to try and give you some comfort." A reunion soaked in whisky and sex. "A shoulder to —"

"To offer to beat Dan up?"

"Well, yeah. Probably. He probably wanted a good beating about then. So he could face himself y'know. But . . ."

"Really? Will you lay a beating on him for me now? A belated Christmas present. A knuckle sandwich to choke on with his eggnog? Hmm?" Lucielle's fantasy made her thoughtful.

Max sat down on the edge of the bed and rubbed his face for a long moment. Lucielle watched him out of the corner of her eye. Was about to go and sit beside him when he looked up. "I should go. They're expecting me at that party. I've got the wine."

"I hit the bottle kind of hard after my non-wedding." Lucielle looked at Max expectantly.

He frowned. "Really?" Max and Lucielle had always been complete boozehounds. He'd heard she was A.A. now. This was the story he wanted to hear but didn't want to hear.

For now he wasn't going anywhere.

"Remember the cottage?" she asked.

Of course. The summers of covert love in the upper deck of the boat house of her family getaway on Pine Lake. "I spent the summer up there. White wine and fruit salad for breakfast. The sun shone every single day. The rangers were terrified of forest fires; patrolled the shore for bonfires every night. They were illegal by the August long weekend." Lucielle realized Max was waiting for her to make sense. "I'd booked two weeks off for the honeymoon but just didn't go back to the store. Dad brought me back down here after Labour Day. Said enough was enough. Got me some interviews but I messed them up.

When I crashed my car —" Lucielle shuddered at the memory of the close call. Max certainly hadn't heard about any car accident.

"Were you okay?"

Lucielle nodded. "I think so. I don't really remember. It was just me and a brick wall at the wrong end of a parking lot."

"A.A.?"

Lucielle shrugged. She had a strange relationship with A.A. "Yeah, kind of. It helps. There's some scary people there though. Alcoholics are fucken crazies, y'know."

"Yeah, maybe. Some strong people," Max said.

"Some nice people, yeah. That's true." Lucielle thought about one of those unacknowledged invitations. The most casual one of all. But fuck it, it was already New Year's — she wasn't going anywhere.

Every single day he was in jail Max thought Lucielle would come and visit. His time inside would have been easier, more heroic, knowing she was out there, in his corner, waiting for him. He never faced pen time, but he fantasized about being face to face with her in the trailer. Conjugal visit. Now, with a stopwatch ticking on the last day of the year he didn't want to know Lucielle had been suffering more than he was.

"Did you get my letters?" Max asked. Lucielle didn't say anything at first. "They're in that drawer. I didn't open them. Mom used to bring them up to the cottage on weekends. She used to bring up these different bottles of wine the girl at the store would tell her about. We'd finish them together in the afternoon, and then dad would barbecue us dinner. I know I should have . . ." Lucielle only realized what this meant now, tonight with Max standing there, trying not to acknowledge his anger or the death of his passion. She realized that life was long and to be lived with the people you knew. But she couldn't articulate any of this. They looked at each other instead. For a long time.

Lucielle shrugged off the comforter and stood. Stretched. She was wearing faded flannel pajama bottoms and a white T-shirt that said Canadian Girls Rock. She walked around the bed so she was behind Max.

His phone rang. "Hello? Yeah I know. Held up for a few minutes . . . I know . . . I know, I'll be there in fifteen." He flipped it onto the desk like he hated it.

"Your party?" Lucielle asked. She opened her closet and considered her clothes.

"Yeah, the party. The party. Sounds like your parents are having a good time. They still love New Year's, eh?"

"Oh yeah."

"What do you know about my case? About what happened last April?" Max asked.

Lucielle snorted like it was an easy answer. "You were fighting in a bar. A strip bar for fuck's sake." Lucielle said with fairly authentic disgust.

"I was looking for that beating I just said Dan probably wanted."

"A what? Penance beating?"

"For what I did — to us."

"Oh please," Lucielle snorted again, this time with slightly mystified disgust. But in that instant she felt she'd learned something about how men think. "But that was, like, a year before . . ."

"I don't know, Luce. I guess I figured we'd always end up together. Forever. So I cheated on you. I know that's a bad thing — I mean, I really know it now. You have a lot of time to think when you're locked down."

"You blamed *me* for cheating you fuck."

"I know, I know. And so we broke up and you started seeing Dan. Fair enough. I didn't hook up with anyone."

"You just fucked someone."

"Next thing I know you guys were getting married and for the first time I couldn't even imagine what the rest of my life would be like. But —"

"But after dropping out of university, dropping out of that e-investors course, falling off that roof doing the framing job, and ending up as a fucking shipper-receiver in that miserable book warehouse. You've been drifting Max, in a downward fucking spiral."

"I know. I know. I guess I figured so long as I had you everything would work out."

"What about the bubble-gum internet business?"

"That's what I was working on when I got arrested."

"Jeez, Max," Lucielle muttered. "Jeezus. So you went to a strip bar. You used to despise those places, man."

"I figured I may as well walk the walk, y'know."

"Try and live up to being the, ah, lowlife you felt you were?"

"Something like that." Max said. He leaned forward and looked out at the apple tree. "I was depressed. Drinking rye —"

"That's a mistake."

"Feeling bulletproof. I felt the urge to, how would you say it, defend the honour of one of the large-breasted servers. A bunch of frat boys were getting pretty rude. My buddy told me to chill out, let the bouncers handle it. But when I told them to apologize — that they ought to be ashamed — they went off. All four of them. I grabbed a knife for back up."

"What, like, a steak knife?"

"No. That would have made more sense. Just a regular dinner knife."

"Can you really hurt someone with one of those?" Lucielle asked, skeptically.

Max turned on the bed to face her. It was obvious she wasn't wearing a bra. "You can if you turn into a drunken, berserk, whirlwind in the midst of four warm bodies."

"Oh."

Max turned back to the window. He looked at the cellphone. "There were witnesses. Plus the frat boys were all white."

"And the waitress?"

"Kind of, you know, Asian."

"Like me only with a boob job, huh?" Lucielle said with more sarcasm she really meant. "Was she grateful?"

"She thought I was nuts. The bouncers kicked the crap out of all of us. They told the police what happened. They all had the exact same story."

"So, how come you're out of jail now?" Lucielle asked.

"I did my time. I was sentenced to fifteen months but I had so much dead time, waiting for trial — dead time counts two for one — that I reached my mandatory soon after court was done."

"You talk so . . . You sound like . . ."

"What?" Max stood.

"Like, you *know* the system."

Max stood as if to go but just looked at Lucielle for a while. She turned back to her clothes and Max reached for his phone. He noticed the stacks of videotapes beside her desk. They reached the height of the desk itself. Empty covers and stray tapes.

"Hey, *Aliens*." Max said. He ejected the tape already in the VCR, found the remote and keyed play; it was at the combat drop scene when Ripley and the Marines leave the space ship to go and investigate the strangely silent colony on the planet below.

Lucielle couldn't decide between a pair of jeans or a nice dress. She took out a garter belt, panties, and bra set all clipped onto the same hanger. Max didn't take his eyes off the screen. She got caught up in the action too and stood with the "let's fuck" get-up in her hand for several minutes.

"I love that part," Max finally said, turning. He almost didn't notice what Lucielle was holding. Did a double take. "Going out?"

"Can I come to your party?"

Max shrugged.

"Oh. That girl you've been having all the sex with is going to be there. She's probably there now, wondering where you are."

Max looked down. Glanced at the screen.

"What's her name?"

"You know her," Max said. "Tracy."

"Tracy? Tracy Persaud?"

"Yeah."

"Well, well, well."

"She visited me every week."

"So now you owe her unlimited cock —"

"It's more than that." Max spoke so simply and mean-ingfully that Lucielle didn't even have a comeback. Max reached out and took the hanger from Lucielle. "I tried to explain it all to you in my fucking letters." He gently played with one of the straps, as if he was curious about its strength but didn't want to damage it. "This looks pretty new." He finally said.

"Yeah, well. You know. A girl can hope."

"Come on, Luce. Don't punish yourself."

"I don't know what it was, Max. I thought I was getting married. I mean, sure if I think about it, Dan and I didn't really know what we were doing. We got engaged so fast and I was on the rebound. It might not have worked out, but I think we both would have worked at it. Y'know, Dan and I had some good times. Just like —"

"Just like we did." He handed the gear back. "Do you still have the emerald green one?"

"The emerald — oh yeah. Somewhere. Do you want to give this set to Tracy? It's brand new."

"No. Thanks. I got her a Christmas present already. Perfume. And a novel. One of those Oprah books. Besides, she kind of filled out."

"Really? She's not a skinny bitch like me anymore?"

"No." Max answered. "And what's up with that? I gotta take you out for a sub. Bake you a cake."

"That'd be nice. A cake that is," Lucielle said. "You gonna put the beat down on Dan for me?"

"Naw. God doesn't want that. He doesn't want burnt offerings."

Lucielle's eyes bugged out at this. "Oh man, you gone Bible on me. Christian? Is that your latest thing, church?" Lucielle laughed at the idea.

"So what about A.A.? That's Bible too."

For some reason Lucielle laughed even harder at this. "You better get outta here. Go to your party." She stopped laughing, "Actually, that's where I was thinking of going tonight."

"You don't want to come with me?"

Lucielle slowly, seriously shook her head. Max's

phone rang again but Lucielle snatched it up. "Hello? Yes, this is Max's cell. Who's this? Uh-uh lover, you tell me first. Oh, it's you Dale. Well this is Lucielle. That's right. Max is here. With me . . ."

Max straightened his spine and relaxed his shoulders, letting his energy pool out around him. His jail muscles blocked out the light and made the wall seem unusually close. He took the phone. "Dale, I know, I'm sorry, man. I'm on my way, I'll be right there. She is? Well, tell her I said what's up and I'll be right there."

7:45

"So guess where our red wine is?" Dale asked the five people lounging on the plush, well-worn furniture. "At Lucielle Drake's house."

"What?" said Hector.

"He said he wanted to stop by — before the year was over," Tracy Persaud explained.

"He probably left the wine in his car, and it's getting frightfully chilled," Elvin said.

"Oh well," said Kim who was kneeling in front of Dale's stereo, trying to activate the turntable.

"Max and Lucy have things to discuss. Sure, a New Year's urge to clear things up," Elvin said reasonably.

"Step eleventeen, make amends," Hector said.

"Is she really in A.A.? I mean, don't you have to drink for years and years and destroy your life before you can go?"

"Come on, she and Max partied constantly all through high school and even more after they became common-law. They breakup, she plans this lavish wedding with some bartender who, wisely if you ask me, gets cold feet, then she hits the bottle and simply cannot stop."

"She has to make amends with Max? *He* cheated on *her*," Kim said.

Hector tried to lighten the mood, "Where's Trevor, he should be here by —"

"She didn't visit him in prison," Tracy said defensively.

No one felt really comfortable discussing Max and Tracy. At least not when either one of them was actually in the room. Tracy had become obsessed with Max once he was locked up. She took one of the weekly visits he was allowed and Max's mom took the other. As time went on Tracy took both visits more and more often. Dale, Elvin, and the others were updated on Max's welfare by Tracy. Everyone assumed Max was pleased with the company, but that things would return to normal once he was out. Normal being something like Max banging Kim's sister Patsy on Wednesday nights while working on his rambling, drinking-man routine the rest of the time.

Instead, Max repaid Tracy with a quiet, attentive devotion. The two were rarely apart. The car that the dinner party's wine was cooling in was Tracy's. She had come with Hector, her brother.

"What about the wine?"

"When are we going to eat?"

"Kim, how much longer will the rice take?" Elvin asked. He was the evening's host. He had organized who would bring what so they didn't end up with six containers of Häagen-Dazs picked up at the convenience store on the corner. Dale's house was the usual gathering place for barbecues and dinners. He'd inherited a sprawling bungalow from his parents. "Kim? Kim, what exactly are you trying to do?"

"Play a fucken record, man. This thing's too high-tech."

"Okay press that — no, the one you had before. That's it. Now hold it down." Elvin even knew how the stereo worked.

"Oh, I get it." Kim mumbled, and Joe Strummer's twang suddenly blasted into the room. Kim lowered the volume. Slightly.

"Hey, The Clash!"

"I haven't listened to these guys in years."

"I listen to them constantly. The Clash and Bob Marley is all I need."

"Is this new?"

"Kim, the rice?"

"Probably another ten to fifteen. I'll take a look at it." Kim got up, pleased with herself and The Clash.

"Okay, listen folks, the night is young, the Merlot and the Fume Blanc are on their way, so I'll make a pitcher of Manhattans to get the juices flowing."

8:15

"Yeah?" Lucielle answered the knock at her door.

"Oh," her mother said, coming in.

Max had his shirt pulled up under his chin and Lucielle was measuring his chest with a dress maker's tape. It was enormous.

Lucielle's mom's eyes glowed with white wine. She wore a gown, low cut with a blue sash and a necklace of lapis lazuli that drew eyes to her collarbone. She balanced a tray with a coffee pot, cups and saucers, cream and sugar, and a plate of Christmas cookies in a way that reminded Max of her bringing Coke and chips to them as kids.

"Crazy huh, Mom?"

"Jail muscles," Max said, pulling his turtle neck back down, embarrassed now that Lucielle had talked him into showing off.

"Yes. Happy New Year, Max."

"Same to you Mrs. Drake."

"How's your mom, Max?"

"Well, thanks."

"She must be glad to have you home." She had deposited the coffee things on the desk, beside the TV — *Aliens* had been exchanged for *Shawshank Redemption* — and was back at the door.

"Uh huh."

"Remember this get-up, mom?" Lucielle asked. She was now wearing the emerald lingerie set Max had asked about earlier. He'd always thought it was magical because of the colour. She got it when she was seventeen.

"It looks a bit tired now, dear." Mother said.

It was faded and a bit frayed around the metal fasteners, the elastic exposed in parts, and conspicuous lime thread closed a few passionate tears.

"Yeah," Lucielle said looking down at it smiling. The loose robe hung off her bony shoulders.

"I should be going," Max said.

To Lucielle's mother the statement made no sense; it looked like they were about to get it on. "Okay," she said and closed the door as she left.

"Have some coffee. Watch the movie. It's so rare I have visitors," Lucielle said tying the belt of her robe. She'd changed while Max kept his eyes on the screen. The room was only so big though, and during the outdoor, night sequences at the beginning of *Shawshank* he had caught the occasional reflection of her in the small screen.

Now she poured coffee.

"Cream?"

"Oh — just a spot. Thanks."

"One lump or two?"

"Three," Max said, then shrugged at the look Lucielle shot him — his taste had sweetened.

Lucielle took hers black.

"We've switched places," Max said, accepting the saucer with his left hand.

"What do you mean?"

"One black, one double double. The doughnut shop at Jung and Ellington." Max spoke in code about years gone by.

"Ah, yes," Lucielle said sitting down and daintily crossing her legs. "Cookie? Help yourself. I live on black coffee now. I usually go down and make a pot about now so Mother obliged."

"Ah."

"What was jail like?"

The phone rang again.

"That's probably Tracy." Max looked at the phone. Watched it ring.

"You should get it."

"Yeah, hello." Max finally keyed it just as the other party rang off. "Shit. I gotta get going." Max sipped his coffee, blew on it and sipped again. Lucielle somehow drained hers and refilled her cup from the thermos flask pot. "Top you up?"

"Sure, one for my baby and one more for the road." Max held out the cup and saucer and Lucielle poured in a few drops.

"Prison?" she asked.

"Jail," Max said, sipping and setting his cup on his saucer. "Jail is where you learn how important the small things are. How important people can be. Friends. And I'm not talking about you or even Tracy. I mean in there. I remember when my first cell partner, the first one I liked I mean, got transferred. We'd been together for three months — he'd been in there for twenty. When he left, it wasn't just me, all the guys on the range said the place wasn't the same without him.

"The days y'know, do some push-ups. Play some cards. Chess if you're lucky. They just pass.

"You ever taken a dump while someone you just met is laying on their bunk, a few feet away? Pure humiliation. Then you get used to being treated like meat. And some of those so called correctional officers are power-tripping Nazis. When you see them come on shift it's just like, oh no. Now what? Lock down? Search? Stress levels go up and the guys start fighting. And *stress*, I never knew the meaning of the word before I went in there. Stress. You gotta stay strong. But you know what I'm saying Luce, being left at the altar like that. In front of all your friends. Jail's just like that, sometimes. Just like that. Look, I'll come and visit you again in a couple of weeks. All right?"

He left Lucielle on her bed with her legs curled up underneath her wearing what was now vintage lingerie. She held the saucer with one hand, her cup in the other.

Max slipped out the front door, he felt bad, not saying a proper goodbye to Mr. and Mrs. Drake. They had been so kind to him, so generous during those teenage years that seemed so far away now. Max and Lucielle had had their own New Year's Eve party in that house. Upstairs in her room. Mr. and Mrs. Drake hadn't minded that they hadn't mingled — hadn't missed the whiskey Max had sloshed into a jar he'd gotten from the shelf in the basement. He knew the family so well back then that he knew where empty jam jars were kept.

The driveway had cars three deep; cars were parked all down the street.

Max had parked half a block away. He knew he'd need a breath of air when he came out of Lucielle's house.

He got into Tracy's car and sat behind the wheel. He didn't start the engine right away. He thought about Lucielle, in her room, on her bed. She still looked like a princess.

9:00

Lucielle finished her coffee and stared. Tim Robbins and Morgan Freeman make it out in the end. Live happily ever after. She watched the sadistic C.O. use an M14 to blast the young inmate who holds the secret to Tim Robbins' character's freedom.

Lucielle sprang off the bed, shrugged off her robe and pulled open her underwear drawer. She caught sight of herself in the mirror and the reflection of her clock radio. "Oh, fuck it," she said. The numbers were reversed, of course. She slammed the drawer shut, opened her closet, and snatched a black cocktail dress off its hanger, and dropped it over her head. Her gaunt body appeared elegant, even classy in a mysterious way. She looked older. Like her mother.

Max had forgotten his cellphone so Lucielle tossed it into a black, beaded evening bag, turned out the light and slipped downstairs. A few of the guests waved to her and called hello as she eased her coat off the hanger in the front hall closet, but her parents were nowhere in sight. She'd left her car in the street when she'd come home from working out that afternoon and now she drove towards the A.A. meeting, feeling more and more relaxed by the minute. Max's visit had been just the ticket.

She pulled over and rummaged through her wallet on a sudden whim. She found Detective Sergeant Keefe's card, turned it over and dialed the number penned in on the back. Message machine. Lucielle hung up. Probably working. Or maybe she'd see the homicide detective with the crooked smile at the meeting.

Lucielle was almost at the bottom of the steps to the church basement where the Denison Avenue group met when Max's cell buzzed. It was kind of neat having a phone —"Hello," she expected it to be Max calling for it.

"'Lo. Max there?"

"Ah, no," Lucy said.

"Who's this?"

"This is Lucy, Lucy Drake. Is that Mr. Diaz?"

"This is Diaz. Lucy who?"

"Lucy Drake, sir. You remember me —"

"Oh! Little Lucy Drake, my goodness, yes. Is my son with you?"

"Ah, no actually. He was but he left his phone with me — by accident."

Lucy had met Max's father a handful of times. He wasn't around much after Max's eighth birthday. Max never talked about what happened between his parents back then.

Lucy stopped on the bottom step, pressing the phone into her ear — a piece of the past — it was a strange feeling on New Year's Eve to be talking to Max's dad.

"Oh. I tried to call him at his mother's last week but missed him. I just, you know, wanted to wish him all the best."

Lucy somehow knew that last week meant Christmas Day. "Sure. I'm sure he'd love to speak with you. He was on his way to a friend's place. Dale, I think. Or maybe Elvin. Do you remember those guys? I've pretty much lost touch with them all so I'm afraid I don't have any of their numbers."

"Oh, no problem Lucy. I'll catch him one of these days," he sounded remarkably sad and, remembering where she was, reminded her of making amends.

"Well, I'll probably see him soon — to return his phone, I mean. I'd be happy to tell him you called," Lucy said, trying to prompt a number out of the old man. But Max's father only asked politely about Lucy's parents then said, "Thank you dear. For all you've done for my son — you and your parents, over all these years, I mean. Thank you. And Happy New Year." He hung up.

Lucy held her thumb down on the "end" button tightly for a long time. But it wasn't the same as those other times in her life when she put the phone down at home and then stood, her hand still on the receiver as it sat on its cradle, connected by wires that went into the wall and down into the ground or up into the sky across the blocks or across the city to the person she'd just spoken to. Like when Dan called, in tears, apologized and said he couldn't really talk. Or when Kim called, the only time Kim had ever called her, and said that Max had been denied bail, that he wouldn't be out that day or any time soon.

A little man in a black suit came out of the meeting room and, seeing Lucielle, politely held the door.

It was packed.

The guest speaker was in the midst of his war story.

"The cop realized how far gone I was. A sack of shit was more sophisticated. Which is what he called me before I took my shirt off. I saw it all in his eyes. They'd been all — all light — full of fire, ready to punish me. A lotta you straitlaced types might not believe me but this was raw street justice, y'know. But this cop's eyes went all soft and mushy when he saw me, all skinny and scarred and tattooed and just pathetic. And I stood there wobbling, telling him I could take anything he could dish out. At least that's what I think I was saying because I knew that's how I thought. I was a punishment sponge. Any filth, any beating, any freezing night I could take, and the payoff was just to suffer . . . and a little taste of alcohol, of course. That was my fuel."

Lucielle wished she wasn't there almost instantly but she knew that was par for the course. Typical. There was a festive mood in the room — the sobriety that had lasted another year for some, or began this year for others, or might finally begin in the coming year for still others — was something extra to celebrate. An enormous chocolate cake was on the table beside the coffee urn. The group's treasurer came over and cut a large piece and put it on a paper plate for Lucielle without her asking.

Extra folding chairs had been set up right by the door and Lucielle sat in one, put her paper cup of coffee on the floor beside her and dug into the cake. A few of the others had dressed up as well.

"And this was a tough cop. He'd been around for years. Down-town beat. Seen lots. But still, that's how he reacted to me. I felt that. I remember it today." The speaker paused to look at his watch; ran a hand through his thick grey hair. "Still, it was another ten months before I gave sobriety another try."

Lucielle glanced at her watch. The cellphone rang again. It made a funny chime, playing some unrecognizable riff; she must have accidentally taken it off buzz mode. Lucielle's first thought was to let it ring, but after getting a few nasty looks she got up and went into the hallway. "Hello."

"This is Keefe; you called."

"Diana?" Lucy asked.

"Who is this?"

"Sorry Diana, it's Lucy. Lucy Drake."

There was a long enough pause for Lucielle to think they'd been cut off. Then: "Drake? From the meetings? I don't think I knew your last name."

"Yeah. I'm here now. I was hoping I'd see you," Lucielle couldn't believe how suddenly this part had fallen out of her mouth.

"Yeah, well. I just got off shift, just came in the door. The machine indicated someone called but didn't leave a mess so I star sixty-nined. Kind of paranoid given my line of work and all."

"I always liked the name of that ah — function."

"Hmm. Oh yeah. So how's the meeting? I know I said I'd be there for sure but —"

"Hey, you gotta keep coming back. It's good. Packed. Feels like a party. There's a cake."

"What kind?"

"Chocolate."

"Mmm."

"Yeah, it's good. So do you think you're —"

"I know, I know, I know. I should. I really should. But I've been out all day and I really need to take a bath. Look, why don't you pop over? I'm in an apartment building two blocks south of where you are."

"Really? Now? I mean —"

"Yeah! It's New Year's. I expected to work late. But something came up at two this morning so they called me in early."

"You've been up since two in the morning? I mean, I don't want to —"

"Hey, it's not like I'm just going to drop off, I need to unwind after a day of —"

"I can dig it," Lucielle said quietly and the two went silent. She could hear the crowd inside laugh at a funny part in the story and wondered if Diana Keefe, who had just been standing over what was once somebody's baby, now all grown-up and murdered, could hear the laughing.

"I could fry us some eggs or something. Hey, why don't you try to sneak some cake?"

"You got it," Lucielle said, her head spinning at this sudden invitation. It was better than she hoped. She thought about the ridiculous get-up she had on under the dress and how that might make her seem. Ah, fuck it, she said to herself. "Hey, if I hurry, I can make it by — oh, it's nowhere near midnight."

"No, it isn't. Not yet." Detective Sergeant Keefe blurted directions, once, and hung up.

Lucielle looked up from Max's cellphone, the meeting erupted with applause and she knew the speaker had just announced how many sober years he had in.

9:00

"Apparently, this bunch of musicians showed up in Hong Kong — Russian musicians — and presented themselves as the Moscow Philharmonic. Tuxedoes and all." Kim told the gang. They were sitting down to eat, finally. Max still hadn't shown up.

"Really?" Tracy asked, eager for something to distract her.

"What happened?" Hector asked.

Elvin's pitchers of Manhattans proved very successful. Kim said hers tasted funny but Elvin explained he made Manhattans with bourbon, not rye. This inspired a taste test and a second pitcher made with Canadian Club followed.

"They played a bunch of shows. Apparently, thousands paid thirty bucks a head to see them."

"Thirty dollars. That's very reasonable for a full orchestra. What did they play?" asked Elvin.

"They must have been good — for people to keep coming — they must have known how to play," said Dale.

"But they weren't the real thing?" asked Tracy.

"The real thing was on tour in Europe that summer."

"Really?"

"That's hilarious." Dale put down his empty wine glass.

"Really quite a hoax." Elvin was impressed.

"The thing I can't picture is getting the band together for the scam. It must have been a conman promoter who knew symphonies. I mean, how do underworld figures find second violinists and unemployed musicians with their own timpani willing to travel? It's not like finding a guy to drive the getaway car or a guy to watch the door of the bank," said Kim.

"Listen to you, as if you could find such people." Elvin.

"Rob a lot of banks, do you?" Hector threw in.

"Well, no, obviously I live a straight life. But if I wanted to find someone to help me renovate the bathroom or do some drywall, no problem. Actually," Kim said, looking around, figuring everyone else was already thinking what she was going to say, "Max could probably find people like that. I mean, if he didn't want to rob the bank with me, he could probably hook me up with a couple of numbers."

"That's true," Elvin said.

Everyone was quiet.

"Funny thing about the Moscow Symphony," someone finally said.

9:00

Max sat in Tracy's car around the corner from Lucielle's. He thought about Dale's party and Tracy's mouth and eyes. He just sat until he noticed that the cold, lifeless, indestructible plastic of the steering wheel had sucked all the heat out of his hands. He turned the ignition. Jazz. The CD automatically came on when he started up. A trio led by some guy named Bill Evans. White boy. Tracy loved his music.

He put the car in gear and made a move. Headed down Balmoral for the party. But at Albermarle Max turned left when he should have gone straight. Spontaneously. Some angel or devil on his shoulder whispering silent directions. It was the music. He drove and listened, realizing he was feeling more relaxed by the minute. That this felt right. The tension that had built before finally seeing Lucielle drained out of him, the way it would if he closed his eyes and really concentrated on letting go when he lay on his bunk in his cell.

The first time he did this was the first time he'd been alone in the six weeks since his arrest. He was in the hole. He'd taken the heat for a sharpened toothbrush found in his cell. No books except the Bible. No canteen. No mattress after seven a.m. Locked in a cell by himself he was able to relax. It felt like heaven. He let go of all his thoughts of freedom and his case, his simple desire for a nice thick book to read, and his complex desire to see Lucielle and give her a hug and ask what happened and to make love to her.

Tracy was supposed to come and visit but that privilege was gone too.

Max drove. Signalling, turning. The tranquility interrupted only by the fleeting anxiety of expecting his phone to ring. But it never did. The pianist started into something familiar. The theme from *MASH*. It took Max's breath away. Transported to the simpler time of endless sitcom reruns. But now that simplicity shimmered like an illusion about to tear: a jazz trio playing a bunch of jazz songs and then this. Not the TV version.

The song ended. The CD ended. It was only thirty-four minutes long. Max hit play and drove through the whole album again. He listened to the theme from *MASH* for a second time in the parking lot of a friend's restaurant. An Italian joint in a flat-roofed, one-storey building near the waterfront. Max hoped he looked good enough in his dress pants and black turtleneck.

The place was packed. The maitre'd looked at him with a charged smile, expecting an explanation as to why he was alone.

"Actually, I'm a friend of —" Max saw his old cell

partner just as he was about to say his name. Sammy was about Max's age, but he'd done way more time and knew the Bible inside out. He looked up, grinned, and came over.

"Hello stranger. I knew you'd pop up one of these days," he said, spontaneously turning Max's handshake into a hug, their clasped hands pressed between their chests.

"Hey, happy New Year, man," Max said. "I thought I should check in, y'know."

"Come on in, bro. You here by yourself?"

"Yeah."

"No problem, we can take care of that. Some friends of mine are having a party." He directed Max toward a large round table surrounded by men and women who looked like they were in a champagne ad; beautiful people, all talking and laughing loudly. The table was covered with plates of food, bowls of salad, baskets of bread, bottles of wine.

"Whoa," Max mumbled.

"Oh, yeah, quiet guy. Right. Look, why don't you sit at the bar."

"That's better."

"You hungry?"

"Yeah, actually I am. I'm starving." Max said, settling onto a stool at the end of the bar.

"Rest easy, man. I'll be right back." Sammy said.

Max didn't catch the signal Sammy gave the bartender but when his scotch and soda came it was a double.

Max placed the tip of his index finger on the corner of the little cocktail napkin his drink was sitting on and pulled it closer, right up under his nose. He raised the glass to eye level in a toast and rolled the first sip around his tongue before swallowing. The bartender nodded, once, and left him alone. Every table was packed and he was kept busy by the waiters who came up for another trayful of trick martinis or imported beer or more bottles of wine. The bar stools were only occupied sporadically. They held single, unspeaking, unsmiling men. Some of them seemed happy, some patiently waiting for something to happen, others just brooded and nursed their drinks. Max was happy.

The guy beside Max finished his beer, put on a pork pie hat, and left.

A waiter came out of the kitchen with a steaming plate of noodles and gave it to the bartender. The two spoke briefly, then the bartender came over and put the plate in front of Max.

"What's this?"

"Farfale with olive oil and garlic. You like hot food, right?"

"Yeah."

"Okay, cause the chef put the hot pepper flakes in just as he finished cooking it. Enjoy."

Max turned and looked for Sammy but didn't see him. He picked up his fork.

A woman with waist-length dark hair came over and put her glass of wine on the bar beside Max's. She took her evening bag off her shoulder hooked it over the empty stool's low back and sat down.

She did most of this while looking right at Max. Max alternated between many things: looking politely back, to acknowledge her as another human being on the planet, trying to eat around the sudden awareness of possibly accidentally slopping food on his chin, glancing at the skin left bare by the open top of her dress and her pert 32As, drinking some more scotch and wondering what the hell was he doing here.

"Max, this is Julia. An old friend from the neighbourhood. Julia this is Max, the guy I was telling you about last week. Remember?" Sammy appeared between them, a gentle hand resting on one shoulder of each.

"Sure, I remember. Happy New Year, Max," she said as if she'd just given Max a present.

"How's the food, buddy?"

"Great. It's delicious."

"Good. I had the chef make it special. You need anything, let me know. I got some tables to check on but we'll talk later — after midnight, okay?"

These last words made Max feel that by accepting the food and the double shot of booze he was obliged to stay and listen to what Sammy had to tell him.

"Sure buddy, I got no place to go." Max didn't know why he lied, but he felt that if things had gone differently at Lucielle's he wouldn't be here.

Sammy disappeared.

Julia sipped some wine and smiled, leaned forward a little, working the dress. Max looked at her sideways wondering what she wanted, deciding that he'd definitely like to fuck her. She looked back, eyes saying he could. She'd come to Sammy's tonight looking for an angle and now, she figured if she took care of this jailbird, then Sammy'd owe her.

"So do you know what Sammy's got going on here?" she asked.

"A restaurant?"

"Naw, this is his brother's gig."

Max forked up more noodles, thinking the gang at

the party might actually be worried. Then he thought: Julia? Tracy? Julia? Tracy? He looked back at Julia and shrugged.

"Whatever it is, he's rolling in it." Julia said. "Rolling in it."

And you want a piece of it, Max thought, with the contempt and distrust criminals often had for each other, not seeing how he fit into it all, just by being there. Sitting on a stool. Eating pasta.

He thought about the all-day lock-ups: twenty-four hours plus in the cell. Sammy sitting on the little desk by the window reading and rereading psalms. He'd get Max to read them out loud. Randomly; trying to see how many, or how few lines it took him to identify it. "Come to my family's restaurant when you get out. It's a nice, quiet place."

Sammy had gotten three months and was shipped to a correctional centre to do his time. He wrote once, when he got out, telling Max to stay strong . . . the days of wine and pussy were coming. Max didn't reply. He threw the letter away. But now, on New Year's, he found that he had not so much consciously memorized the restaurant's address but had mentally photographed it. He was able to picture it, clear as day, staring back up at him from the steel toilet bowl.

Max ate his noodles and swallowed more of his remarkably satisfying scotch and soda, feeling better, having spoken with Lucielle, feeling confident since they had not fallen into bed together — although thinking about her now in her *Penthouse Pet* get-up started to give him a hard-on. He took another sip, willing the booze to wash away the guilty relief he felt from not being near Tracy Persaud — who was, literally, his saviour.

Julia was arguing with the bartender about what type of red wine he was going to refill her glass with.

Her fingers, long nails painted gleaming white, stretched over the rim of the glass. A few drops of wine stood out on the back of her hand. "Not that heavy Portuguese shit. I was drinking Merlot. Sammy gave me a glass of Merlot. It had a big L on the label."

The bartender, all powerful, was amused at her protest and was a second away from pouring wine all over her wrist, knowing it would run down her forearm and drip off her elbow onto her dress.

"Give her what she wants," Max said.

The bartender paused. Then did as he was told.

Julia smiled at them both victoriously.

"What time is it anyway?" Max asked.

"Five to. But my watch is five minutes fast," Julia said without looking at her watch.

"'Who gives you work and why should you do it at fifty-five minutes after eleven,'" Max quoted.

"What? Who said that?"

"The Clash." Max said holding up his glass. They clinked rims.

"To us," Julia said.

Whatever, Max thought, and poured scotch down his throat.

10:45

"I think they're the best band of the century," Kim said.

"What do you mean of the century? Rock has only been around for fifty years," Hector argued.

"You know what I mean," Kim said. "And it's not just their integrity but their energy."

"I saw them back in high school."

"Really?"

"Yeah. The Combat Rock tour, back in Ottawa."

"Cool."

"If you listen to that live album that came out a few years ago, the sonic unity of their playing is completely transcendental."

Everyone started laughing.

"Okay, you're cut off, Kim."

"I'm not drunk!"

"I mean from DJing."

"Put on — what's Trevor's favourite album? Transcendental?"

"Blues. Transcendental Blues. Where's Trevor anyhow? I assumed he'd be here," Kim asked.

"Don't you know?"

"Let's check in with Mr. Trevor," Elvin said. He picked up the phone and dialed. He waited a moment then said, "Yes it's me, who else would be calling you? Oh, that's good. An apple fritter, eh? Sounds delicious. Not much really, everyone's here, except Max, who's gone AWOL. Yeah, she's here. A pitcher of Manhattans. Two actually, but that was before we ate. Yes, I trust you. You want to say hi to anyone? Maybe later? Of course I'll be calling later. Bye Trevor."

"An apple fritter? Where is he? A doughnut shop?"

"The Coffee Time in the heart of beautiful Parkdale to be exact."

"What? Why? What's he doing there?"

"Wishing he hadn't been so sure about the Leafs beating the Sens in the playoffs."

"Last spring?"

"Sure. We'd gone into that Coffee Time and got into a bit of a jag, insulting everything about it in a horribly snobby way. The smell. The regulars. The mediocre coffee —"

"So why'd you guys go in there?"

"I needed a coffee. I was hungover. Very hungover. Even then I had to go back and upgrade to a double double, their brew is so foul."

"So what about the bet?"

"Well, I must admit," Elvin looked at all of his guests, "I freely admit I ultimately felt revived by that coffee so in deference to the spot I said I imagined that some of the regulars are probably in there at the stroke of midnight on New Year's, and there's no place they'd rather be."

"Y'know, that's probably true."

"So, that weekend the Leafs/Sens series began and Trevor was shooting his mouth off and the Sens swept the series and now he's down there with my cellphone. He has to put Kwan Lee, the night manager, on as soon after midnight as he likes, then he's allowed to come over."

"*Allowed* to come over."

"That's what little brothers are for."

"He's not coming," Tracy said, surprised she could speak without crying.

"You must be depressed, honey. On New Year's Eve. What a bastard," Kim said.

"Not depressed. Just sad. And Max is no bastard. Just — just mixed up. He's not necessarily with Lucielle right now. Who knows where he is."

What do you mean? The question hung over the empty plates glistening with expensive olive oil. Serving spoons stuck out of half-full platters, each person had an array of red wine, white wine, and champagne glasses before their setting.

"When Max was arrested it was easy for me. I guess my personality leans toward faith and devotion — blind devotion. It's funny how intimate a visit in that filthy crowded visiting area can feel. Real intimate. I feel I helped Max through something. And I needed him, too. I always knew where he was. That he wasn't fooling around. Not like — like now.

"I knew this was coming. Just not tonight." Tracy covered her face with her hands but still didn't cry.

Hector put his arm around her. "Hey, come on, it's Max we're talking about. And — and I agree he and Lucielle had some things to discuss. But he is not fooling around with her, no way. Max and me had a long talk about that last week. I know him and —" Hector ran out of optimistic steam.

Tracy looked up. "How many times did you visit him in jail?" Everyone went quiet and looked sheepishly away from one another. "That's what I'm afraid of. Max is wild. He ended up in jail, right? Well being in jail changes people."

"Not Max."

"Yes. Max too. He's human."

11:55

"Hey Sammy. What was that prayer? Prayer of offering?"

"Oh yeah: 'I place myself entirely in your care. I hand over to you my self — my mind, memory, will, emotions, body, sexuality . . . I ask you, Father, to fill me with your

Holy Spirit and all the gifts and fruits of your Spirit.' That's the fucked up thing with that prayer. You shouldn't ask for anything back. God is love. It's a given. It's there for all humanity. It's just plain ridiculous to ask for it. Our job is to give. Give everything to God. Period. We must empty ourselves and let God fill us up." Sammy noticed a very well-dressed man with grey hair come in, a woman half his age in a micro dress on his arm. "Hang on a sec." Sammy wound his way through the crowded restaurant to greet the newcomers.

Max and Julia looked at each other. "What a guy," Max said.

SHROUD

The Holy Shroud of Turin. Jimmy taught me about it.

I watch Aunt Marlys make up her son's funeral suit. My mother helps.

"Jimmy wore this to Anita's wedding."

Mom finishes going over the jacket with a lint brush. She holds it at arm's length, turning the hanger, inspecting. My aunt takes a crisp white shirt off the ironing board. She holds a green silk tie to the collar. "He insisted on wearing this tie." She puts down the green one and holds up a deep burgundy one. "I still prefer this," Aunt Marlys turns to Mom for her opinion.

I wasn't at the wedding last spring. I haven't seen Jimmy in a couple of years. "I won't be at the funeral tomorrow." I stand up. "I'm going up to spend the night up on Bear Head's Point."

"Dress warmly," I hear Mom call in the distance.

I've never been up here in October. The trees are bare. You can see for a distance. I build a fire. Bigger than it needs to be. I have to keep my distance for comfort's sake. When it's produced a solid bed of embers, I gently place Jimmy's bush hat onto it.

There's a good photo somewhere of Jimmy when he was nine. It's Christmas and he's wearing the floppy camouflage hat for the first time, his dad smiling blurrily in the background. That was before Aunt Marlys and Uncle Travis split up. Now with Jimmy gone, Aunt Marlys is pretty much on her own.

The hat burns down to a skeleton of heavy stitching. And then that's gone too.

I know that I have a lot of wood ash in the mound on my camp shovel but I don't want to leave any of the hat behind. This has to be done properly. Using my flashlight, I pick my way down from the point. The sky will begin to lighten soon. I tip the shovel and a breeze pulls off wisps that fly along above the rushing water. A twist of my wrist and the rest follows, a grey cloud hits the water and vanishes.

Back at Aunt Marlys's house there's a girl sitting on Jimmy's bed. She's about seventeen, eighteen. A woman. We nod at each other. I go into the kitchen. Marlys always has a pot of coffee on. Eventually, it occurs to me that the young woman must have been Tina, Jimmy's girlfriend. I'd never met her.

"How was the point?" Mom asks, lighting a cigarette.
   "Lonely," I say, reaching for the pack.
   "You're gonna miss your cousin," she tells me.
   "What about Aunt Marlys?"
   Mom only shrugs after a long silence. We're due over at my sister's house for dinner. Her kids must be getting big. I wish I'd brought something from the city for them.

Aunt Marlys introduces Tina to me, then wanders off. I didn't realize there'd be so many people at my sister's house. My brother-in-law hands me a Labatt Ice, pats me on the back. As if it means something.
   "How was the funeral?" I finally think of something to say to Tina.

"Did Jimmy ever tell you about the Holy Shroud of Turin?" she asks.

"Sure."

"He always wanted to see it."

Maybe he's seeing it now. It's too corny to say out loud. "I saw a documentary not too long ago. They say Jesus spent all this time in India."

"Yes. I think I've heard that somewhere."

I'm a little surprised. How many people actually think about this stuff?

"Yeah. From when he was twelve until he was thirty. Anyhow, he became a yogi or enlightened Buddha or something."

"Ah," Tina says, as if this explains everything.

Outside, the forest stretches into the distance. My sister carries the first steaming pot from the kitchen and puts it on the dining room table. How my sister and her husband can afford such a big house is beyond me. But I want to finish speaking with Tina. Now. Before we're called to sit down and it's too late.

"Apparently his life energy was so powerful, so acute, that when it left his body it actually changed the molecular structure of the cloth touching him."

Tina hesitates for a moment. Maybe she thinks I'm talking about Jimmy. "Oh . . . oh? Really?"

"Uh-huh."

"Did you ever tell —"

"No. I should have. I was going to but —"

But he got wasted and put himself and his car around a tree at two in the morning. He might have been coming from Tina's house, I'm not sure. It was one of the first really Fall-like nights of the year.

Du Maurier Summer

The summer after high school, Joe got a job landscaping. Times were good for the industry and he worked seven to seven. The boss made him an informal crew chief; he drove one of the trucks and learned how to price jobs. He made shitloads of money and got really depressed.

The sun would fall and he'd spend the evenings out on the verandah of the suburban house he'd lived in since he was three. Clutching a Bic lighter. Sipping beer that went warm two minutes after opening. Mumbling curses about the neighbours as they strolled past. Sitting with his head in his hands.

His brother would be up in his room, listening to the first three Venom albums. Over and over again.

This was the summer of their parents' second youth, rediscovered love. They were hardly around. If they weren't out for dinner, or sailing a rented boat, they were at a friend's cottage. They discovered festivals: bluegrass, strawberry, antique. They went to resorts. Canoeing by day, watching stars by night.

Joe knew his whole life was ahead of him and wanted to rip himself out of his skin. He couldn't stand any of his friends. Couldn't stand not being at work.

His brother worked way fewer hours at a video store in the north end of town. Watching bizarre foreign films on air-conditioned weekday afternoons. He wasn't like his brother. Joe's brother wasn't popular at school. In the hallways and at assemblies, out in the smoking area, Joe saw his kid brother as a liability.

Now his smoke wafted up into his brother's room, Venom crankshafted down. Joe knew his brother was up there jerking off to porn mags. He knew he should go up there and tell him to knock it off. He knew he should call up Sarah for a date this Friday and see if she had a friend for his loser kid brother. But instead he slumped back down into one of the Adirondacks his parents had picked up from a guy who made and sold them beside the highway up north. Joe slid back and brought his hand up in front of his face, Bic pointed directly at the end of his cancer stick.

In the moment the lighter sparked a buddy from the football team, pedalling by on a mountain bike, recognized the briefly illuminated face.

INVERT AND
MULTIPLY

———————

"Will you respect me in the morning?"

"I don't respect you now."

"Okay, knock it off, you two," Mr. Sanderson said, coming over to the cluster of desks at the back of the room. "And get your books out. Where's everybody else? What about Lily and Chris? Where's Everton? Jerome? We should have started by now." Sanderson realized he was pestering the kids and turned his back on them.

"Everyone's late," Billy said, referring specifically to Mr. Lal, the other teacher. He unzipped his backpack and took out his book. Janelle was looking at him.

"It must be true," she said.

"Shh," Billy hissed.

"But he just asked about them. He must have heard — something."

Billy gave her a vicious shrug, tense from the rumours and doubt. He looked at Mr. Sanderson's slightly slouched back. He was okay. He just wanted the kids to do well in school.

Janelle took her binder from under her chair and opened it. It was the biggest binder anyone at Trudeau Memorial Secondary had but it held a disproportionately small number of pages; especially since it was almost December.

Mr. Sanderson looked at his watch. He looked at the

door and Jerome walked in followed by Mr. Lal and Ms. Sikorsky.

"What's up, what's up!" Jerome greeted Janelle and Billy.

"Hey dread."

"Got a spliff?"

He sat down a few desks over and took a handful of loose, unorganized paper out of his bag.

Sanderson smiled at Sikorsky. She was a volunteer. An undergraduate finishing a B.A. in analytical geometry, planning her application for teacher's college, counting on the time she put in this class, and Sanderson's referral, to help her out. "Okay. You know what you're doing from last week?"

"Actually, I was hoping I could work with Billy today, for a change."

Billy's face brightened deviously. Janelle shot him a look.

"It's okay if I work with your tutor?" Billy asked Jerome. Jerome was the most serious student that Billy knew so he didn't want to tread on him.

Jerome looked up from the mass of writing on the page he was studying. He still hadn't figured out what class it was for. Maybe it was one of his inventions or a screenplay idea. "I don't care who I work with. I just want to make sure I know this stuff." He gathered up his sprawling pile and dumped it on a desk beside Janelle. Janelle took out a cellphone and started scrolling through recently called numbers.

Sanderson looked at his watch again. Three students. Two teachers and one tutor. No sign of Lily, Chris, or Everton. The two other students, the Nguyen twins, were on the sick roll: food poisoning. A lot of students in the school were ill. Sanderson was preparing the three-month report he and the principal had agreed on in August. He sighed, wondering what that meant for his extra help program.

Mr. Lal went to the big desk at the front of the room and put his briefcase, a graduation present from his mother, down. He turned, then, realizing the desk was already covered with Sanderson's files, marking, and fragments of lesson plans, he turned back and put the briefcase on the floor.

Lal approached the cluster of people at the back of the room as if undecided about his willingness to participate.

Sanderson had recruited him at the staff meeting the week before Labour Day. The principal had acquiesced with a wave of the hand, moving the meeting along without letting Lal speak. Sanderson had smiled briefly, glanced back at the paper in his hand, then asked the teachers seated between them to pass it down to Lal. It was a copy of his own résumé.

Lal had always pictured himself teaching to a crowded room. The students rapt at his crystal clear explanations of the quadratic equation or analytical geometry. This school wasn't quite where he'd hoped to work. It was near the area, but the students were very different. The administration was strict, which he'd always hoped for, but in a way that didn't seem to work.

Now Sanderson looked at his watch then looked at Lal shaking his head. He went to his desk and sat down without saying anything.

Billy and Sikorsky were setting themselves up a few desks over. Jerome was still looking through his non-existent filing system.

"I knew I should have skipped this stupid no-help

class," Janelle said, glaring right at Lal.

"Then you'll never learn this stuff and you'll be stupid your whole life," Jerome said without looking up.

"I'm not stupid."

"Oh yeah, I forgot, you're beautiful."

Janelle stifled a smile at Jerome's weird sarcasm and looked back at Lal. "Well, when am I gonna use it? Tell me one job where I gotta know how to do fractions — except being a teacher."

Lal felt his body becoming warm. Janelle's blond hair was yanked up into a ponytail at the crown of her head, a white bandana swathing her hairline and forehead, right down to the bottom of her ears, which sprouted absurdly huge hoop earrings. He was sure she was in one of the gangs the teachers speculated about in the staff room. "Well," he began. He hated this question. "Carpenters and renovators still measure —"

"Renovators! You think I'm gonna be a renovator?"

"Miss Danier, this *is* the twenty first century and —"

"It's not cause I'm a girl —"

"You're a girl?" Billy asked.

"My brother's a renovator. At least he was till he cut his thumb off running a radial arm chop saw."

Lal had been hoping Sanderson wasn't listening, but now everybody had stopped working. "Really?" The surprise and horror turned his voice into a medium-sized squeak.

"It was at a cottage on an island. He had a thirty-minute boat ride before they could start driving him to a doctor." Janelle's voice had grown quiet. She looked at the phone and tossed it onto the desk.

Sanderson had drifted over. He had his hands in his pockets, his shoulders relaxed. His body language exuded sympathy. Lal stepped back and leaned on a desk, putting his hands in his pockets too; but his efforts to emulate Sanderson only made him seem overly detached.

Billy had heard the story.

Sikorsky looked through her wire-framed glasses, her expressionless gaze lingering on each face for the same amount of time.

"What kind of saw was it?" Jerome asked.

"A radial arm chop saw," Janelle said quickly. She suddenly felt there was nothing to this story. Wished everyone would go away. "Makita makes the best ones," she spoke quickly, "but my brother's was a De Walt." She began to draw quickly on the first page in her binder. It was blank. The ellipse of the blade, elegant tubes of its rails, the embossed protractor base, and the operating grip with its trigger and red safety button all fell together into an exquisite sketch.

"Wow, that's real spacey looking, I've never seen one of those things."

"They cost seven hundred bucks," Billy said.

Lal couldn't get over Janelle's artistic ability. He was taking life drawing at night school at the college on the other side of town. It was an effort to jump start his love life, but he was aware of a steady improvement since the class began. Not even the instructor drew with Janelle's effortless precision. He looked at Jerome, who was still studying the drawing. Why couldn't he express his ignorance with as much confidence as this kid? Head full of dreadlocks, ring in his nose.

"Is your brother okay?" Sanderson asked.

"Worker's comp sent him to some computer class. They gave him a special keyboard."

Sanderson looked at the wall at the back of the classroom. The teacher's thousand-yard stare. Janelle watched him go back to his desk, wishing the story had more of an ending. She looked back at Lal and her face hardened. He cleared his throat and sat down.

Billy thrived in small group environments. He was already dividing fractions and beginning to feel like he knew what he was doing.

"Don't forget to cancel," Sikorsky said.

"Where?"

"The three and the twenty-seven."

"I did — oh, like that. You can do that? Even though I already cancelled the twelve to get the three?"

"Yep. Cancel all the way down."

"Okay. Before we continue I need to understand one thing," Jerome said.

Lal looked at him expectantly.

"Why can't we add fractions with different bottom numbers? What's the problem?"

Lal felt himself getting warm again. "Well you can't. It would be like adding apples and oranges." In teacher's college moments like this had come up, had been discussed but then someone always made a joke, like it wasn't really anything to worry about.

"That's another thing. Why not? You got some apples, you got some oranges . . . you have a nice bag of fruit."

"Fruit salad," Janelle said.

"Okay it's like this," Lal began again. He paused, waiting for some perfect example to pop into his head and flow off his tongue. His students waited too.

"Hey dummy," Billy piped up. "Say you work in a restaurant. You have one pie cut into six pieces and another pie cut into eight pieces and you need to tell the kitchen how much pie you have. What are you gonna do?"

"Whattaya talking about?" Janelle interrupted, her voice showed both contempt for Billy's understanding of this stuff and an eagerness to actually have it make sense.

"They're both partially eaten. How you gonna figure out how much pie the restaurant has?"

Jerome jumped in. "I'm gonna point at each piece and say a number as I go. It's called counting you —"

"That's a negative. The pieces of one are smaller then the other," Sikorsky answered gently, heading off Billy's exasperation. "But you know, guys, I'm not sure if this example is really that clear or —"

Jerome had stopped, finger in mid-count, eyes up at the ceiling, not blinking. "Ohh, I get it. Do you get it?" he asked Janelle.

"Don't get it, don't care, just wanna pass the credit." Janelle gave up on trying to understand. "It's not like I'm ever gonna use this stuff."

"It's very simple," Jerome said. He picked up his cheap mechanical pencil and looked at the question.

"We make a good team," Billy said, smiling shyly at Sikorsky.

"What are your friends up to?"

"Ask them for yourself," Billy pointed the end of his pen at Jerome and Janelle.

Sikorsky looked over at them. Jerome smiled. Janelle met the volunteer's eye and looked quickly away.

"Not them. Everton. And Lily. And what's his name, the desperate one?"

"Chris," Janelle answered before she could stop herself.

"Where are they right now?" Sikorsky turned on Janelle.

"Dunno," Janelle shrugged.

"They're around someplace," Billy explained.

"Maybe they got food poisoning," Jerome said. "Maybe you should check the hospital." This shut Sikorsky up. She couldn't tell if Jerome was joking.

"You're almost ready for decimals." She turned the page in Billy's textbook and saw that only the review quiz remained.

"Decimals are a breeze." Billy dismissed them with wave at the book.

"Percents?" she asked.

Billy grimaced. "What does your husband do?"

Janelle kicked Jerome under the table and he nodded, almost imperceptibly.

"Not married," Sikorsky answered.

"But you have a boyfriend?"

"I guess you could call him that."

"I see."

Lal was tuned in, too. He looked at Jerome and Janelle; they seemed preoccupied with their word problems.

"So how old are you anyhow?" Billy asked.

Sikorsky looked at him. Her expression hadn't changed since she came into the room. She didn't tell him, or tell Billy they should get back to work, she just looked at him and waited.

"You don't have to answer that. And I don't mean to diss you. It's just, since we're working together like this, I thought we should get to know a little bit about each other." Billy waited for a moment, knowing Sikorsky wouldn't say anything. "So tell me one thing, when last did you go out with this guy you call your boyfriend."

"Last night."

"What did you do?"

"Pizza. Movie."

"And afterwards."

Sikorsky didn't answer right away.

Lal could see she'd set herself up, thinking the kid wouldn't push so far. She should have shut the kid down right away. He would have. But she had to learn.

"French vanilla cappuccinos," she said finally. She waited one beat, just until Billy opened his mouth then said: "At my place."

"Ah, I see." Billy blinked. "Then?"

"Then what," Sikorsky snapped. Billy hesitated. Confused by those perfectly poker-faced eyes. He wanted to play professional hockey and his mind did a flip, applying the physical limits he pushed himself to on the ice to what he was doing now. For absolutely no reason.

"Then did you —"

"That's enough!" Lal yelped, suddenly gripping the sides of the desk. He cleared his throat. Jerome and Janelle both laughed, heads back, showing off top molars. Jerome slapped the top of his desk with one palm. Sanderson wondered what was going on. "This conversation is entirely inappropriate." Lal glared, unsure who he should be disciplining.

"You. You shouldn't be prying, asking such questions with the marks you're getting. And you," he turned on Sikorsky, "you really will have to be taught to conduct yourself in a more professional manner." Lal fought to keep himself from looking in Sanderson's direction.

"Jerome, what did you use as the L.C.D. in the third question in row four?" He tried to normalize things.

"Ah, forty-eight."

"There's a number smaller than that that three, four, and eight all go into."

Billy gave Sikorsky a conspiratorial look, as if they'd agreed to something.

"Let's get back to work," Sikorsky said, nudging Billy's notebook towards him.

There was a thump on the outside of the door. Voices, a nervous laugh, a curse, as someone struggled to turn the knob even though it wasn't locked. The door flew open, slamming against the wall, and the three missing students fell into the room.

Lily Anderson straightened, her hand still on the knob, looking directly at Mr. Sanderson as if he was the last person she expected to see. Everton McKenzie went directly to the back of the room, unslinging his backpack and extracting his books, acting eager to get the extra help the class offered.

"Mr. Sanderson," Lily said, but the third student, Chris Hayes, sweating like an alcoholic outside a liquor store before it opened, grabbed her sleeve and pulled her back towards the unoccupied desks.

Sanderson watched them. He glanced back at the open door; Jameson, the custodian, was going by like clockwork with that enormous broom of his. "What's up, teach?" he greeted Sanderson, thumping his chest with the top of his fist. "Want that closed?"

"Thanks Jamey."

The custodian, who was the same age as Sanderson, leaned into the room, grabbed the doorknob, looked suspiciously at the latecomers, and pulled it shut.

"What's going on?" Billy asked.

"Nothing."

"We'll tell you later."

"Shut up. There's nothing and nobody to tell."

"Mr. Sanderson," Lily said. She still had her coat on. Her hair was wet. Sanderson hadn't noticed it was raining.

The other two were making a great show of opening binders and flipping through textbooks. Everton even had his highlighter out.

"Mr. Sanderson. If anyone asks, could you tell them we've been here since the start of class?"

"Lily!"

"Class is more than half over," Sanderson pointed out.

"I know sir, but we *wanted* to be here on time."

"We'll stay after. The full dose," Everton volunteered.

"That's right, so it'll be exactly as if we were here the full time."

Sanderson squinted at Lily, then jerked his head at her desk. She took her seat with the others. Lal and Sikorsky stopped working while the newcomers got settled. Sanderson didn't reassign either of them right away, didn't say anything. He studied his report standing up, as if he were about to stop at any moment and come to the students.

Sikorsky noticed Jerome looking at the other three. Janelle was trying to find out what was going on, using some ridiculous sign language that was annoying Lal. Jerome was staring at Chris, then shook his head and picked up his mechanical pencil. He had started working on a fresh sheet of paper that he vowed to keep in its own section in his binder.

Billy looked grim. His face was set, as if he was about to attempt something very difficult.

"Shut up," Lily hissed at Janelle, who sighed and rolled her eyes.

Sanderson finally approached. Hands in pockets. "Has your teacher introduced decimals or are you still on fractions?" He asked Lily, Everton, and Chris. "I know you're here for fraction help."

Lily looked at him plaintively. So did Everton actually. He knew he'd let them stew long enough. They'd opened their books but were too unfocused to actually start checking answers. He was deciding whether he should ask Lily what was up, or just hope the class ended without interruption. The students would leave and he would drive to the grocery store with the list he and his wife had made between toasting bagels and getting the cream from the fridge and clean mugs out of the dishwasher.

Sanderson heard the door open but he didn't turn around right away. Whoever it was certainly wasn't expected. Hadn't bothered to knock. He watched the faces of his students. His co-workers. A man in a slightly baggy suit walked in with a careless swagger. Looked them all over.

"Meigs," he barked, once he decided Sanderson ranked.

"I remember you," Sanderson replied. He didn't introduce himself. Didn't offer his hand. Meigs hadn't offered his. He was all business. "Hiding in the last place you thought we'd look. Right under our noses." It was clear who he was talking to. "Yeah. Half of the division is out there looking for you. Turning over rocks. Knocking on your mommy and daddy's doors."

The three students were shaken by how quickly they

were busted. But they stayed solid. Silent. Everton's hand shook slightly in his lap.

"Someone recognized you, Chris. You were made at the scene." The cop was gloating mildly. It was a good day.

"Officer —"

"Sergeant," Meigs corrected Lal.

"You're mistaken. All these students have been here since class started. Almost forty-five minutes now." Lal was a superb liar.

The cop looked at Lal like he was contemplating dragging him out behind the school and putting a bullet in his brain. For some reason he turned his gaze on Sikorsky, the other person in the room he didn't recognize. She'd looked away when Lal spoke but now she looked back up, meeting his gaze with such frank intensity he figured she must be the undercover rumoured to be working the school. Meigs turned to Sanderson, who was staring at Lal.

Lily looked at him too. Guiltily.

"Mr. Lal you're mistaken. These three just arrived. It's the other three who've been here since the bell."

"Aw, Sir!"

"Shit!" Everton said. "Shit, shit, shit!" This would be his third time in Y.O.

Chris was the only calm one. He sat up very carefully in his seat, then began to bend, reaching down to the battered grey gym bag he carried everywhere he went. But it wasn't where he put it. Jerome had hooked the strap with toe of his shoe and pulled it over to his side of the desk. Now he sat back, his legs stretched out, feet planted comfortably on the bag as if it were his own.

Chris looked at Jerome, the cold glint in his eye fading into sadness.

Meigs raised his hand to his mouth and went to speak into a tiny walkie-talkie he pulled out of nowhere.

"Don't call your buddies," Sanderson said. "Don't worry about handcuffs. They'll go with you."

Chris, Lily, and Everton all stood — as if Sanderson were in charge. Not Meigs. The cop pouted for a second, then put the walkie-talkie away.

Later, when everyone was gone, Sikorsky lingered at the edge of Sanderson's desk. He'd sat down and hadn't moved, hadn't spoken since Meigs had escorted the accused out.

"You should have lied," she said. "I would have backed you up."

Sanderson finally looked up at her. He looked exhausted. Older than his thirty-five years.

It was the end of the day.

Sanderson thought about the grocery list for a long moment. "Do you want to get some coffee?"

"No," Sikorsky said.

BATTLE AT SEA

1 : Midway

I'm eleven and I'm learning about the Battle of Midway. I spent all summer reading about Operation Overlord, and just when school started I got an amazing graphic novel called *Turning Point in the Pacific*. I loved reading about aircraft carriers and their giant elevators that took planes to the enormous hangers below the flight deck. Way cooler than *Star Wars*. Now I'm reading the book the movie with Charlton Heston was based on. Actually, I think the book came after the movie; it has pictures inside of Heston as Admiral Halsey. I've already seen the movie twice. I watched it again tonight on the TV in my parents bedroom while my sister and her dumb friends did stuff downstairs.

It's about one-thirty, so I'm reading by flashlight. My parents finally come home from the dinner party at the Muise's. Mom comes to check on me right away. I pretend to be asleep and when Mom pulls the door shut it blows her smell over to my nose. Mom smells nice, like nice food and cooking and the perfume she put on when she got all dressed up.

My dad comes upstairs and I'm actually falling asleep when the sound of their arguing comes down the hall and into my room.

I think about Ensign George Gay, the only member of his Torpedo flight to survive, but I don't think about him for long. Midway was more than fifty years ago. I get up, the cool air coming through my pajamas feels more better than the coziness of bed. It feels more like the air in my parents room must feel. I open my door and peek out. Across the hall and down a bit, the door to their room is closed. I can picture their stiff bodies though. Their voices are low but really, really tense. I have to be careful because they might come out and go downstairs where they can speak more loudly without worrying about waking me or my sister up. It's horrible. I can feel it in my throat. Mom wants Dad to say something, to talk about something; I don't know what, something at the Muise's dinner party maybe. The Muise's don't have any kids so I don't really know who they are. Dad just wants Mom to shut up. I can tell that just from the sound of his voice.

Suddenly, I turn and go back to bed. I don't know how I decided. I guess I just wanted to listen to the radio, so I put my Walkman on and put the radio on really quietly so I'll be able to hear if someone comes into my room. Under the sheets I click the flashlight back on and look at the movie photos of the war.

The next day is Sunday so I sleep in. Mom makes bacon and eggs every Sunday and I can smell it cooking. My zombie sister is already in the kitchen, talking on the phone. She's good at that. She leans over in the corner, out of the way, peering out the window.

"Got some leaves to rake, boy," Dad says. I'm the last one up. That he's sitting at the table reading the fat weekend paper surprises me for some reason. But where else is he supposed to be? I look from him to Mom over at the frying pan. Mom's watching me and I realize I've stopped in the middle of the floor like my brain went dead or something.

There's two guys in my class who fight all the time.

They've sworn to kill each other and I know one day it will happen. The whole class is divided into whose side you're on. But sometimes, like on the field trip to the Science Centre, no one really cares.

Dad looked up from the paper, "And after the leaves . . ." Dad left it to me to finish.

"The Bills are gonna destroy, ah, Tennessee!" I say. Dad and I have watched football every Sunday since school started. He turns and looks out the window, studying the job ahead. There're still lots of leaves on the trees so they'll have to be raked up again next Sunday. I've always thought raking should be done once, after all the leaves are down. Mowing isn't a problem, just go right over them. But Dad doesn't agree.

I drink my whole glass of juice in one go. My sister isn't saying anything and something makes me think she isn't hearing anything at the moment either. She's just watching us all from her corner. Her juice isn't touched and there's a piece of toast with one bite out of it on her plate. She's a freak. My Dad notices she's watching us so she looks back outside and starts mumbling into the phone. All her friends are dumb. I don't know what they talk about.

"Did I show you that picture of the pilot, the only one in his whole squadron to survive?" I ask my Mom. It's a famous picture. Sort of like a team photo, all the pilots in their flight suits standing on the deck of the Hornet. He's usually circled, the one who made it.

"Ah, I'm not sure, honey," my Mom says. She turns the burner off and starts using the spatula to put fried eggs onto the plates stacked beside the stove. Then I remember: my flashlight, my book version of the movie *Midway*, and my Walkman were all on the night stand when I woke up. I look into my Mom's face, but she's a zillion miles away.

"What are *you* going to do today, Mom?" I ask.

She just puts the plate in front of me without making a sound.

2: PRESS GANGED

Helen Karapakakis was our secret weapon. We'd recruited her only two weeks before the talent show. Actually, Raj, our guitar player, did. Herb, the singer we'd formed the band with, had become really rude; he kept having tantrums, saying he wasn't going to sing and that Jimmy, the drummer, and I had to practise more on our own time because we made a lousy rhythm section. But we all knew what his problem was. I, for one, did nothing but play bass when I wasn't doing homework or reading about war.

Anyhow, Raj showed up with Helen at one of our rehearsals. Actually, he'd called me and Pinky — that's what I called Jimmy — in for a special Wednesday night rehearsal to help get ready for the talent show. I got permission from my mom and she even drove me over to Pinky's house on her way to her boyfriend's. I went around the back of the garage to the back door. It was never locked.

Our amps were on either side of the drum kit, facing it. The mic stand was directly across from Pinky's kit so we formed a wide circle. When we played, everyone looked at each other. The whole set-up was on an old blue rug Pinky's mom had found at a garage sale. She was always concerned that we'd get cold, and couldn't get over how much time we spent out here.

At first, I thought Raj had just brought Helen to

watch, even though she was flat-chested and never spoke. This was cool, since no girl I ever told about our band was ever interested. We were just too nerdy and too crazy. Crazy because we played death metal, the really evil stuff. Well, covers at least. We usually practised on Saturdays and Sundays, then maybe on some weeknights if we could all make it.

Raj plugs in and asks me and Pinky what we're waiting for. Instead of saying "Herb," which would have made perfect sense, Pinky and me look at each other and get up off the long couch under the window, the one his Dad watches football on while he's not working on dirt bikes and snowmobiles for extra money.

We get ready. "Captor of Sin," Raj says. Cool, that's the heart of our protest. We weren't going to waste time warming up, playing scales faster and faster, or on one of Raj's homemade songs. They all had dumb lyrics but we didn't have the heart to tell him. Then, to my surprise, and Pinky's surprise too, based on how big his eyes got, Raj turns to Helen and holds out a sheet with a column of lyrics printed on it that he just finished unfolding. "Need this?"

"No. I memorized it."

This is what I noticed right away. Herb could never really memorize anything. That was his big problem as a singer. He couldn't quite remember the words. I was the only one who always seemed to know exactly what came next. I could start singing right in the middle of a lot of songs and sing right to the end. So Raj decided I should help Herb and they got me a mic for back-up vocals. But I can't really sing so it sounded like someone was talking in the background all through the song. It ruined everything and sometimes I felt like crying because it was my fault nothing worked. But Pinky liked it and used to laugh and said I should talk like that through every song. He said it was original. Without Pinky there, I probably would have cried. So I thought, *Wow, she doesn't even want the page just in case.* Then I realized she had come here to sing with us.

"Wait a minute," she said, and took her red cardigan off. No tits at all.

Raj counted in and we started to play. Helen started to sing but we stopped almost right away because the mic was so high Helen had her head tilted way too far back. She folded her arms and scowled at the floor while Raj fixed it. Then we started again. She was way better than Herb. Loud and ferocious. I would have been embarrassed to yell so much but it sounded good. We had to do it again because, well none of us were warmed up and we were all busy watching Helen sing and listening to her voice and how it sounded with our playing. I made at least three really big mistakes.

"Captor of Sin" was a fast song and Raj was a really good guitar player. He was surprised when he learned that Pinky and I listened, I mean really listened, to death metal and insisted that we start a band. Herb had the most music of any one I knew. He bought stuff. He borrowed it and burned it on his computer. He knew where to find unreleased albums on the net. All kinds of stuff. He listened to music constantly, and knew a lot about rap, nu-metal, and even some jazz. I think he really wished he could rap but he couldn't. Not at all.

When he heard we were starting a band he pretty much insisted he be the singer. Since no one else had said they wanted to sing he just became the singer. One of our first rehearsals was on a weeknight in November. It was the first day it snowed. Winter had arrived but Herb insisted on singing in Pinky's garage without a shirt on. We were his audience.

Helen was in my English class but she never really said anything. She'd just moved here, and showed up at Trudeau Memorial a couple of days after Thanksgiving. No one I knew had become friends with her — she usually wore a lot of black mascara and had really bad posture. I remember once she said the Bar Mitzvah movie scene in *Duddy Kravitz* was "incredibly insightful and really cool." Our teacher didn't know what to say to that. She got good marks. At least I assumed she did — maybe she was flunking. I had no idea. Her notebooks were covered with really good drawings of horses and giraffes. It never seemed weird until I thought about it at rehearsal that day. Horses and giraffes in big crowds. Or close-ups of one horse's head and one giraffe's head talking. Like something on the cover of one of Pinky's dad's magazines. But what do horses and giraffes really have in common?

"We have to do it again, Helen. Is that okay? I don't think I told you but sometimes we just play the same song over and over until we get it right," Raj said after the third time.

I don't think we'd ever gotten any song right. We'd just hacked around. Raj had been serious, but not that serious about the band, and then we got this four and a half minutes in the talent show.

We did "Captor of Sin" again. Helen had turned the mic stand around and she just stood there, facing straight ahead at the inside of the garage door and screaming like she was on fire. I stayed facing Pinky; actually, I moved right up close to the kit — the position I usually took when it was just the two of us practising. Raj roamed around in the wide space left on the night-blue rug. The band had changed.

The fourth time was perfect. Right at the end of the second verse, before the solo, Raj and I looked at each other and did a little jump at the same time. It was perfect. Perfect, perfect, perfect.

It was only after we finished playing and I was towelling the sweat off the neck of my bass that I remembered Herb. I figured we'd just keep Helen a secret.

"What about Herb? Is he sick?" Pinky asked. Raj became sinister. He went over to the far end of the empty work bench and took the phone off the wall and, slowly pulling up the antenna like he was going to hurt him with it, brought it over to Pinky.

"I was waiting for one of you to ask. Call him and tell him he's out."

"What?" Pinky was shocked.

"We have a new singer." Raj nodded over at Helen who was sitting on a stool by the back door, waiting to go. She had her red cardigan on again. It was actually kind of cool in a *I'm in disguise* sort of way. She was staring at a calendar of girls in tight, torn-up T-shirts holding different tools. Wrenches and hammers and stuff.

"I can't call Herb. He's not out of the band." Pinky started laughing like Raj was joking.

Raj sighed and made a really weird sound. I realized it was his back molars scraping. It would be cool if he did that into the mic. He moved his feet a little like he was getting ready for someone to try and push him over. "We only need one singer and she has a way better memory."

Two things that were true. Raj kept holding the phone

at Pinky but he acted like what Raj was saying was insane.

I came over and took it. Dialed. Raj was right. We'd never done a perfect song before. I'd never done anything perfect.

Raj watched. "I found her. For the band. So one of you should —" He looked at Pinky then at me.

"It's ringing," I said. "Herb, it's me. I'm at Pinky's . . . We have a new singer . . . We just had a rehearsal and she has a really good memory . . . Helen . . . Yeah, Karapakakis . . . She sounded good to me . . . I think girls *can* sing Slayer." Pinky said something and Raj laughed. Something about Slayer's original singer being a girl I think, but I'm not sure. Herb was pretty upset. "Well, she didn't forget anything . . . I don't know, it was Raj's idea . . . Because we wanted to try Helen out . . . She's really good . . ." Then, I copied my father, word for word, for the first time in my life. "Why are you yelling?" I asked. It was weird because whenever my dad said it, I felt like my mom had every right to be yelling. "We *are* still friends . . . You wouldn't do that, Herb. You're not a snitch. I know you wouldn't do that . . . Maybe you can still be in the band as a back up —" I looked at the thing in my hand and pressed the end/talk button.

We were all quiet. Then Pinky said, "I'm pretty sure the very first singer for Slayer was a girl." Raj and Helen smiled.

"Tom Araya is just a fill-in," Raj said, and we all laughed.

"Fuck Herb," Helen said, still laughing. She was looking right at me. I didn't say anything but I didn't look away. Finally she glanced at the other two.

"Yeah," Raj said. "Fuck Herb." But I could tell he didn't mean it.

At Trudeau Memorial no one could do anything. Girls couldn't wear tops with spaghetti straps — no one could wear T-shirts with beer names or pot leaves or even skulls. Instead of a Christmas pageant, like in grade school, we had a solstice pageant that didn't represent anything other than the shortest day of the year. During Ramadan, the kids who were fasting were treated like outcasts. They had two separate tables to sit at in the caf and teachers usually asked them why they were in the caf at all. Our math teacher explained that they would be held responsible if a kid ate, but there was no way they could actually restrain a kid from eating. Pinky asked why the school didn't have any Muslim teachers.

None had applied.

No one seemed to believe him.

"Black History" month was changed to just "History" month so no one would feel left out. We talked about the railroad and compensation for the descendants of the Chinese workers. We talked about Vimy Ridge, which was at least halfway interesting, and the class listened to the story I had read about a veteran who became a bank robber after the war and was killed trying to escape from prison.

During the talent show auditions we played a song by Rush about trees. Mr. Lipowski said it was a good metaphor, and an appropriate choice for Trudeau Memorial. Raj had got us to play it slower than normal too: an original interpretation he called it. I think that since we were sort of outcasts who had suddenly shown an interest in something the school was organizing helped to get us into the talent show. Pinky and I especially —

all we did was go to class and go home. No teams. No clubs. No school spirit. No idiotic pack of friends. Pinky and I liked to joke that we were liable to show up with shotguns and that everyone was a little scared of us.

Once we were on stage and plugged in on the afternoon of the talent show, we were going to blow everyone away by playing "Captor of Sin." As a protest. Raj's brother was going to help us. He was in his last year and working as part of the stage crew went towards his Theatre Arts credit.

We bought two of the biggest, cheapest white bedsheets we could find and Pinky and I sewed them together into one gigantic flag. We sat in the garage and started at opposite ends with spools of thread and needles from his mom's sewing room.

There was a stereo above the workbench that had been pieced together out of mismatched components as the one in the house was upgraded. The TV was up there too. Pinky's dad didn't work on motorbikes that much anymore. He sold the last one for a digital camera and had gotten more and more into doing stuff on the computer. He was trying to make a visual family tree for all the relatives.

We listened to early Metallica records and tried to figure out why old people were so boring and uncool. Sometimes we didn't talk for long periods of time.

Raj dropped by with Helen. I wondered if they were going out. Pinky kept looking at the two of them, but I don't think he could tell either. Raj went on and on about how much Metallica sucked now and exactly when and on which album they went wrong. He really liked Vader and finally went home to get some of their CDs for us to listen to while we made the banner.

Helen stayed with us. It didn't seem like any big decision that she wasn't going to tag along with Raj. It was neat having her there, since she was part of the band. She watched us really closely for a while, practically staring, but it didn't bother me. Then she took out a black hard-covered sketch book. I imagined we were sailors on a ship, far out to sea, on a voyage we had been forced to go on. Press ganged. There had been eighteen thousand men in Nelson's fleet at the battle of Trafalgar. I'd just learned that. Press ganged sailors always made the best of it. They had to. Especially on the day of battle.

"What are you drawing?"

"A horse," she replied. "With a giraffe's neck and head."

"Why's that?" Pinky asked.

"So it can see over the jumps." Helen's sarcasm came out like she couldn't help it. It was how she talked.

"Do you have any brothers or sisters?" I asked.

"Yeah. But not in this town. My mom has two kids with her husband. Not my dad. But they're a lot younger than me."

"So your dad lives here?" I asked.

"My godmother," Helen said after a while. It was like she'd been drawing a very difficult part and wanted to concentrate. "I live here with my godmother. Her name's Agnes. She grew up with my mom but she doesn't have any kids. Well, she has me, now."

I could tell Pinky was about to ask about her father but he saw my face and didn't say anything. I spoke instead. "I live with my mom. My folks are separated. My sister, she's older, she lives with our dad."

"I know," Helen said to my surprise. "I know who your sister is. She's nice."

My sister and I pretty much never spoke anymore. When I called my dad and she answered she either immediately put him on the phone or told me she'd tell him I called. I thought about it again but I couldn't picture Helen speaking with anyone at all in school. Not in class, not in the hall, not in the smoking area, nowhere. She barely looked at us when we were at school. For the first time, I thought Pinky and I should go over to the Fish and Chip shop on East Street behind the school where everyone hung out.

We were supposed to meet in the middle but I sewed a little faster. It kind of scrunched up at the spot where we met; I wanted to do it again but Raj said it didn't matter.

The next night I got the biggest surprise yet. We went up to the schoolyard, our old grade school since it was closer, and stretched the banner out on the ground.

Raj's brother was supposed to come and spray paint on it but when he showed up he had a whole bunch of his friends with him. Including my sister. She had gone to live with our dad at the end of last summer. Now it was spring, almost summer again. It had stopped raining and the fields weren't too muddy anymore. I hadn't talked to my sister much all winter, especially since Christmas, when she'd gotten drunk and made mom cry. All she and mom did was fight. No one could tell my sister what to do.

It turned out that most of the people there were on the soccer team, and they went ahead and started up a little game.

Raj's friends had all kinds of spray paint, not just black, and were excited about "Doing up" our flag, as they put it. They stood around the sheet and asked us what we wanted. I think they were a little freaked at the sheer size of it. Raj and Pinky both surprised me by mumbling "I dunno." They seemed embarrassed by having all these older kids standing around, asking them what to do. I ended up doing most of the talking. The artists seemed to like my ideas. They were simple enough, and they had some good ideas too.

My sister and I stood and watched. "How's mom?" she asked.

"Fine, I guess. Derek took her to that fancy new Chinese place for dinner last night."

"He take you?" she smiled, knowing the answer.

"Nope." For the first time, we laughed together, at mom and her boyfriend. I didn't mind being left on my own so much. But my sister hated mom for letting Derek leave us out. "How's dad?"

"Okay. His latest squeeze is really loud though."

"Really?" I blurted.

"Don't get any ideas. They'd never get it on while you were visiting." Her directness saved me from having to make up some excuse for being excited about actually hearing our dad fuck someone from his office. He had a long affair with an out of town client. That's what broke him and my mom up. Then that fell apart and it seemed, from what my sister told me, that he just dated whoever now. "Mostly it's about sex," she'd told me on Christmas morning. She'd taken three long swallows on a rum and coke, like it was lemonade in a heat wave, then added, "So it never lasts."

"So you guys could get, like, totally expelled if you actually do this." She turned to face me, made sure she had my gaze. She looked a lot like our mom. Only my sister had a nicer body. I guess since she was younger. Not that I think about my mom or my sister like that. Just noticing. My sister seemed really tired. I got the feeling just then that if she could run far away from me and Trudeau Memorial and our family she would. In a second. "A lot of people don't like, well, Satan and all that. It offends them."

I couldn't believe that she knew about this. I'd always pictured her face, in particular her shocked face, in the crowd of students when our band exploded into one of Slayer's greatest songs. Doing Slayer had been my idea. I said we owed it to the music and no one could argue with that. It was who we were. It was where we were from. Deciding to not do this was never an option. At least not for me.

She didn't say anything else. We stood together for a while longer. She actually pointed Helen out to me. She was coming around the corner of the school. The far corner, near the parking lot. She was with a guy I'd never seen before. He had long black hair. Down to his waist. I assumed they were coming over but a few minutes later I noticed they'd stopped partway out into the field.

Helen was talking, pointing people out. She pointed my way. I nodded back, trying to be cool, and the long haired guy actually smiled and waved. I felt good. Like Helen had told the guy I was cool or something. I looked around later and Helen was gone.

My sister handed me her can of beer to finish and went to play soccer.

The flames looked really cool.

Pinky came over. "It looks great!"

"Yeah," I said. "But there's no way it's gonna happen. We probably won't even get to play."

"Why not?" Pinky was surprised.

"It's not a secret."

"But look at this," Pinky waved his arm. Our banner was stretched out on the pavement between the basketball hoops. One girl, her shoes off, was kneeling near the centre adding finishing touches with emerald green. Pinky and I moved slightly and got a good look down her top. Her bra was neon blue. The others were standing around the sheets, drinking from cans of beer, talking quietly. One guy was holding a spray can in one hand, beer can in the other. He was wearing a mask over his mouth and nose with two big round filters sticking out of it. Someone said he had allergies.

Three people were sitting, smoking, around home base under the new chain-link backstop. In the field my sister emerged out of the pack, running desperately on a breakaway. The goalie charged out from between the sweatshirt and jean jacket that marked the net and dove before she could shoot. He knocked her down as he grabbed the ball and, rolling, leapt up and threw the ball further than I could kick it. My sister got up, brushed her hands off and jogged back down the field.

"This is cool," I said.

"Hey, who gave you the beer?" Pinky asked.

III

Raj's brother and the girl with the blue bra stayed late at school on Thursday night putting the banner into place. Their teacher trusted them. They told us she went home to get high with her husband who was an economics professor at the university.

The talent show was on Friday afternoon. A group of girls did a dance routine to some hip hop crap. Pinky and I figured their big ambition was to dance in the background of some wannabe's video. They all did the same thing, made the same moves at the same time. Went from being in a straight line to a big V shape to being in two rows and then back into a straight line. They wore snap pants and tight white T-shirts that showed the straps and hooks of their bras. I guessed they were all wearing thongs too.

Oscar Bley and his friends made up a little rap about Trudeau Memorial. His DJ was actually really good. He should have entered the show on his own. I thought of asking him if he wanted to come over and jam with us but metal bands with scratching always lost some of their heaviness, sounded too mish-mashy. Too bandwagony. A couple of times during Oscar's rap he set up rhymes and little scenarios that were perfect for curse words but he always went into some funny direction that didn't even rhyme. Pinky looked at me with a *phew* that I didn't understand at first. Then I realized, if Oscar had gone off the deep end and done an Eminem our protest would have seemed lame and really annoying. But Oscar would never do anything like that. He didn't have the balls.

Raj caught my eye and waved us backstage.

As we worked our way through the crowd, Jimmy.com grabbed my sleeve. "Is it true? You guys are gonna bum rush the stage with some death metal shit?" I just pulled free and smiled and shook my head.

Mr. Lipowski gave a little speech when he introduced us. Mostly he talked about when he saw Rush perform "Trees" and joked about being pretty wild or stoned or something. Nobody believed him or his grey goatee.

I could tell all the students were curious to see what we'd do. Everyone knew what was up, they had to. I sort of didn't understand Lipowski's introduction — it was as if he didn't suspect anything.

We came on after Robbie Panzer, who did stand-up that was mostly impressions of the teachers. It was predictable but he was good at it and everyone laughed their heads off. He was a tough act to follow. I noticed that one of the guys who'd helped us paint the banner was at the board and I thought, *Maybe this* will *work*.

Raj was cool. He put on his guitar and checked *everything*. I was plugged in and turned on and just wanted to play. Pinky was nervous, too. Raj had told Helen to come out last, like she was running out and taking over the band was the effect he described.

The banner fell too soon.

Raj's brother had attached weights to the bottom so it would fall fast and evenly, he'd used a fancy theatre word for the effect but I don't remember it. I'd told him we wanted it to unroll but he said it wouldn't unroll. It would drop.

The banner dropped. It had that upside down star — I don't really know what it actually means — and a big 666 on it. The blade of a broad sword went through the loops of each numeral, weaving them all together. Flames licked the star across the bottom and up the sides of. Fuck Trudeau Memorial and fuck all the efforts at being so perfect and balanced. No religion? Fine. No culture? Fine. Here's Slayer!

I panicked and started to play, fast. "Captor of Sin" is a fast song and Pinky followed me. Raj whirled around and made us stop with a flat karate chop to the air and a huge frown. The banner shook a little in the centre. Someone was behind it, ruffling it. I could hear Helen swearing and Pinky started to laugh.

Raj had both his hands in the air like a conductor

only he had a guitar pick in one hand. Finally, a set of fingers with chewed down nails and silver polish grabbed at the bottom and Helen appeared, bent over, hoisting a handful of sheet up over her head. Standing up straight she ran straight for the mic. She'd shaved all her hair off and painted a wide band of black make-up right across both eyes like a mask. "Captor of Sin!" she yelled, giving everyone on the planet the finger. Raj looked back at Pinky and me, gave one big nod and all four of us started the song properly.

Pinky said Helen sang like she was barfing up bullets. I don't think she ever changed notes and somehow she put just as much power, which was a lot, on every single word.

We got to the end of the first verse and chorus and still hadn't been unplugged. Raj and I did our jump right before the guitar solo perfectly, without looking, and just kept playing our faces off. I was lost in the song, forgetting about the crowd and the protest and Trudeau Memorial. I looked at Pinky, whose face was all twisted since he was playing so fast, but I could tell he was happy. I felt something pressing my shoulder and expected to see Ellsworth-Jones the principal, or worse, Wells, the boneheaded gym teacher, but it was Helen, pressing the back of her shoulder against the back of mine, the way rock stars do. She was pounding her fist in the air. Looked at me, eyes flashing behind her raccoon mask; that's what I thought of at the moment, a raccoon. She zoomed back to the mic stand, jumping over the coiling wire of my bass and Raj's pedals as she went. Her happiness and her energy reminded me of the little kids in the playground behind the daycare in our old grade school.

My sister told me afterwards that the soccer team and

their friends had formed a ring around the sound board and were cheering our song wildly, pretending not to see Ellsworth-Jones and Wells and the other who were trying to get to the controls. Then she told me, with even more excitement, that when he found out I was her kid brother, the team's goalie asked her out.

Raj's brother and his friend stood at the stairs leading onto the stage from the main floor and politely told the teachers trying to get to us that Mr. Lipowski had introduced us and to please wait till we were finished to make their announcement. They said they acted as if everything were going according to schedule, despite the fact that we were ripping the air apart with total black magic. Fast and loud.

Wells finally got through to the board and started yanking cables. Raj and I went first, then Pinky's primaeval drums suddenly sounded like small toys — but for some reason, a lot more real. Helen fired "Behold" into the mic but the final "Captor of sin," was just her regular voice. My ears were ringing a little, we'd never played through anything as loud as that P.A. before. Then I heard the students cheering. I was near the edge of the stage and Pinky ran out from behind the kit and flung his sticks into the audience. Helen was giving everyone the finger again and screaming, "I fucking hate you all. Die, die, die!"

"Freedom is a six six six," Raj said, looking back over his shoulder at the banner. The fingers of his left hand still had a chord pinned down and he was turning a pick over and over with the fingers of his right hand. It was as if he was letting a new riff develop in his imagination before playing it.

I saw a towel sitting on the floor near my feet. It was

mine but I had no idea how it got there. The principal and some of the teachers were on the stage now, coming toward us from all directions. Helen was acting insane. One of them grabbed Pinky's arm even though he was just standing there, not running away, not playing the drums, not doing anything. He looked scared. Someone grabbed at me but I yanked my body away and picked up the towel to the dry the sweat off the neck of my bass. But it wasn't wet at all.

3 : JUNO BEACH

Somebody was writing on my arm. I didn't even realize it until the second numeral was done. Sarah was talking to the person with the squeaky, stinky black marker. "One. Yeah, three-sixty-one" — my entrance and registration. As if someone would just walk into this milling crowd of stripped-down, soon-to-be swimmers. Some shaved and greased up. Others jumping on the spot, shaking the natural, at-rest tension out of their wrists. A few rubbed their bellies uncertainly; this morning's O.J. is supposed to kick in energy from last night's oversized pasta, but the engine doesn't seem to be working right. Nerves. Nerves, of course. It's a triathlon, after all.

Sarah says good luck. Kisses my shoulder when I forget to offer my lips. I go towards the tight crowd at the water's edge. These people are much more still; raw physical power shimmers in the air around them. Swim, bike, run. Eager to start. I turn and wave back at her, flash a big smile, reminding myself to try to put her at ease.

We won't last, Sarah and I. She thought my triathlon aspirations were championship based, I trained so hard. But when we checked in last night, the lobby was full of lounging iron men. And women. All of whom could go further on less oxygen than me. You could tell just by looking at them. They weren't necessarily more muscular than me, but there was a certain bigness to their energy, a deeper silence to their relaxedness. Simultaneously more and less. How could I beat that? I lived on coffee and heavy metal headphones — Sarah and I met at a Void of Emptiness concert. But I never wanted to win. I wanted more.

The gun went. Or someone yelled "Go!" I didn't hear them but we started to move. Jostling and jogging forward, splashing into the lake. Ankle deep. Then knees. Some wading on oblique angles looking for a blank space to launch and begin front crawling across the water. I waded through the pack, waited for a space to clear in front of me, still facing directly across the bay. Then, leading with my hands, thumbs parallel, I dove, smacking neatly onto the water's skin.

I always knew I'd become physically active at some point, I just put it off as long as I could. Reading about war, playing in the band. Finally, in the summer before my last year of high school, I bought some free weights at a yard sale. Started swimming at the community centre to get my cardiovascular up. Pinky's mom bought a new used car and gave her old clunker to him. He was happy to pass his bike on to me so I stopped taking the bus.

No one in my family really struck me as particularly fit. Not even after that day, years ago, before I was in my first band.

We were camping. Mom had made sandwiches out of the stuff in the small green cooler and we spent the whole day down at the beach. My parents read and swam. Splashed around really. Cooled off. My sister and I played and swam. We used to play together a lot back then.

The beach filled up after lunch as more and more people came down from their campsites. Some teenagers played wildly frantic volleyball down at the far end. Swam out to the raft beyond the buoy line and took turns pushing each other off.

Families loaded into canoes and paddled out into the middle of the big, dark lake. Looked back at the shore. Turned and paddled around the island that was in the distance. Another family came and set up their towels kind of close to us. It was the only spot left that was big enough for them, but I thought it ruined the mood for me and my family. Both my parents waved, nodded hello. It turned out Dad had noticed their campsite a few rows over from us, on the way to the comfort station. He asked them something about the lantern he'd seen in their campsite. How could it be so small yet so bright?

They had a boy a little older than me who had a big Tupperware box *full* of toy soldiers. When he dumped it on the sand beside his enormous *Star Wars* beach blanket, I just had to go over and look. I think my sister rolled her eyes and took out an *Archie* digest. She liked Veronica and said if Archie married Betty he'd end up beating her. He wouldn't be able to help himself.

The boy, his name was Devon, handed me a tank. It was small and I didn't think it was supposed to be any kind of real tank but it was really detailed. The ridges of the tread, the smaller barrel of the machine gun sticking out beside the cannon, the engine grill — it looked really real. Devon started lining up a platoon of soldiers so I drove the tank over and blew them all away. Then he reached into the pile and took out some sort of assault helicopter, with little rockets under the stubby wings and everything. Tank buster!

"Ambush!" Devon yelled, and blasted my tank.

Time stopped when we played with that set of soldiers. It was incredible. Those toys went so deep. My sister came over and played for a little while but didn't really know how and got bored fast. Devon kept telling me how cool his toys were, and I totally agreed.

"And you don't have one of those lanterns either," he looked right in my face and smiled. This made me feel funny. I wasn't sure why, but his mom looked away from her book, not at us, but she was distracted by what Devon said. I just looked at Devon and shrugged. We went down to the water and played D-day. Devon had never heard of Juno Beach. His dad brought the Tupperware box over and put it upside down in the sand — in from the shore line a little. He put artillery pieces — this set even had two sizes of artillery pieces! — on it and said it could be the bunker complex we had to capture. Went in for a swim. That was when it started.

My mom and dad and sister had been in the water just a little earlier. Horsing around, my dad throwing my sister, my mom gasping and laughing. Then dad had gone to the lengthwise rectangle of buoys and swam up and down. Like a fish. He could even go up and down like a dolphin, only faster.

It turned out Devon's father could swim too. And Devon immediately told me his dad was better, faster, stronger. "He can hold his breath for, like, five minutes and just swim underwater." Okay, maybe. Whatever.

When his dad came out Devon asked him if he wanted to race my dad. "Sure," he said and looked at me. I got up and ran over to my family's little area, our campsite away from our campsite and told dad. He said no without even thinking about it, or looking in my face. "But," I said and pointed at where Devon and his dad were down by the water. "Too lazy!" Dad called, explaining with a friendly wave, and Devon's dad waved back and nodded. Grown-ups do a lot of waving and nodding. I always thought it was an important thing and looked forward to doing it when I got older.

So Devon and I went back to Juno Beach and his dad went to lie in the sun. "My dad would have won," I mumbled, even though I don't know why. Devon looked at me. After that our playing wasn't the same. Devon went on and on about what a good swimmer his dad was and I just blanked him out. I found myself just staring at a man, looking at the belts of bullets and the machine gun, imagining the death and violence on Juno Beach.

Devon got bored too. He swam a little. Kept talking even when I didn't answer him. He talked to himself a lot. Splashing around. Doing a basketball play-by-play that didn't make any sense. I sat on the shore. Put all the soldiers back in the Tupperware box and put them beside Devon's Boba Fett towel. When I put the toys down, Devon's father thanked me in a way that made me mad.

My sister showed me an *Archie* where Reggie and Veronica end up with pies in their faces. I thought their faces looked mean. I liked Jughead usually, but today I just imagined him bleeding. On Juno Beach. Or at Dieppe. I'd forgotten about the disaster at Dieppe until just then. That's where Jughead would die.

The sun was getting low, turning everything orangey, and my parents started talking about going back and lighting the barbecue. Mom wanted us kids to go and take showers after dinner. Tomorrow we'd drive out somewhere to buy milk and bread.

We started gathering our stuff. "Oh, what the heck," my dad said. I looked up. Devon's dad was standing with his hands on his hips. Friendly, but challenging. Dad looked right at me. Then mom, who was smiling. They really loved each other.

Dad walked down to the water and Devon started

cheering and jumping up and down. They stood at the water's edge talking about how to do this. The moms stood too, folding their arms and smiling politely. Out beyond the buoy line to the anchored raft. "And back." Devon's dad suggested. "And back," Dad agreed like it was obviously a good idea. I was afraid he'd get tired. A lot of people had already left the beach, the smell of barbecue wafted down to us. Smoke from campfires drifted out over the water from a couple of primo lakefront spots. But the people who were still on their towels realized what was happening and looked over to watch.

Dad and Devon's dad walked out until they were in to their waists. Halfway to the line of white buoys. "Go!" Devon's mom shouted and they plunged in, hands first, wrists together, both of them. They easily crossed the roped-in swimming area, ducked neatly under the buoy line and came up on the far side without losing a stroke. Side by side, all the way out towards the raft.

Devon screamed and cheered. "He's winning. My dad's the fastest!" He was, too. It was hard to tell as they swam away from us, but Devon's dad reached the raft, grabbed it both hands, held on for a second for an extra breath, which I thought was cheating, turned around, and pushed off.

"Hey soldier boy," my sister sneered, "watch this." I thought she was talking to me at first, but then I realized she was speaking to Devon. I don't know how she knew Dad was such a good swimmer. It started when he reached the raft. He didn't grab on at all. He just kind of disappeared, his feet coming up and over — heels, feet and that was it. He shot towards us, getting closer by the nanosecond. Arms blurred, buzz sawing the water. Not breathing. Feet hardly splashing at all. He zoomed past

Devon's dad, fast as a shark.

"Wow," Devon's mom said. "He's really fast. Is he a police diver or something?"

"He's still got it," my mom said, quiet but happy.

"He was on the national team, dummy," my sister said to me, before she picked up her beach bag and left.

Dad swooped under the buoy line and came right towards us, finally rising in a falling cascade of water, once again in knee-deep water. "I wasn't sure I could go in a straight line without my goggles," he said. Devon's dad splashed in, still going like someone might snatch second place. He stood up, gasping and laughing. He thought being beaten so badly was really funny. I think I learned something from that man that day.

They came over and roasted marshmallows after dinner.

I never found out where Devon got that toy soldier set even though I asked for it for Christmas and for my birthday the next two years running. The third year, I asked for an electric guitar.

Now it was my turn to rear up in knee-deep water. I'd moved steadily through the pack by pulling alongside the person ahead of me, pacing myself for several strokes then sprinting ahead. I was definitely in the first third of the herd, but swimming was my strongest event. On training days I liked to swim last instead of first. I could always find more reserve energy to burn when I was in the pool.

Ahead of me, a loose crowd of officials, coaches, boyfriends and girlfriends — including Sarah — lined the exit point. Swimmers strode ashore and jogged to their bikes. I was carried along by the crowd, the press of energy behind me. Sarah was there, stopwatch around her neck. There was a big hill in the distance. We had to race over the smaller hills to its base, dismount, and run up it. The finish line was somewhere yonder. I glimpsed back at the lake, emptying its swimmers. This was only my second triathlon, but I'd already decided that this moment, this view, was my favourite part.

SEMPER FI

Johnny Hotrod had a hard-on for the devil. Went around town in a jacket with six six six on the back. Upside-down star and everything.

So when Johnny saw the devil in the laundromat on Bathurst, he went in, grabbed him by the horns, and slammed him face first into the operating instructions he'd been reading. They were on the inside of the washer lid, laid out in two columns of white block letters.

Johnny kept slamming the devil's face until syrupy black blood was smeared all over the instructions. Then he changed directions and slammed the devil's face into that plastic thing in the centre of the machine — the thing with wings flaring out at the bottom that sort of two-steps back and forth, getting your clothes clean. The agitator wasn't very durable — from a battering ram point of view — it cracked, splintered before Johnny could get a nice rhythm going. Johnny slammed the lid down on the devil's back — dramatic, yes, but he knew it wouldn't really hurt. Johnny Hotrod stepped back, breathing heavily.

"Motherfucker. Think you're evil? Ain't nothin'. I'm Johnny Hotrod and I'm takin' you out, fucken panty-waist!" Johnny had just finished a stint in the army. Everyone in his platoon thought they were evil. Bat-winged skull tattoos. Doing time in the brig for flipping-off officers. Showdowns with strip club bouncers who were ex-army themselves.

The devil carefully put his long taloned hands on the

edge of the oversized washer and prepared to push himself back into a standing position. The reek of his own blood (which he'd never actually smelled before, and was in fact a little scared by) and the overripe scarlet capes he'd put in the washer had him close to vomiting. He'd been caught off guard, but now he prepared to unleash a Satanic counterattack that would level this side of the city.

Johnny saw the lid of the washer begin to rise so he put his head down and charged like a bull. He machine-gunned kidney shots — a technique he'd perfected over hundreds of hours on the heavy bag — breathing and pounding rhythmically, like a piece of mid-century factory machinery. The devil's kidneys went from tender to bruised to ruptured. Alarm bells went off in Satan's brain.

"Motherfucker." Johnny gasped, sweat pouring off his face, dripping from his forearms. To him this was just a workout — the devil wasn't even fighting back. Sure enough, the Antichrist collapsed into the narrow aisle between washers. He moved slowly on the cracked, dirty tiles. Faintly, and with great effort.

Johnny looked around; he'd never been in this laundromat before. A college student was quickly transferring wet Gap clothes into a dryer. She was a science student. A geneticist who, years later, in her mid-fifties, was destined to perfect a procedure that would cause humanity an unprecedented amount of grief.

At the very back of the laundromat, a prostitute wiped her lips on the back of her hand. A corpulent man was doing up the fly of his three thousand dollar suit, waiting for his knees to stop feeling like jello. He and Johnny locked eyes; they seemed to recognize one another.

Outside, a kid walked by, peering uninterestedly. "I'm right around the corner," the kid said into a cellphone.

Johnny turned and put the boots to Satan. Kicking, like a bronco at first, then carefully picking tender spots and swinging his leg like a soccer player. He stomped the devil's throat, kicked in the back of his neck, ground a heel into his balls and screwed it back and forth. Johnny told the devil he was pathetic, that he dressed funny. "Am I evil? Yes I fucking am!" he sang. Johnny grabbed the devil by the lapels of his shiny devil suit and pulled him to his hooves. Spat in his face. "Turn it on motherfucker. It's do or die!" Johnny desperately tried to remember his regiment's war cry but couldn't; he was too excited. "Ortona, Reichswald, Hill 812!" He screamed out battles from regimental history instead.

The devil recognized the places, these events, and came back to life. A little. He shook his head to clear it and swiped at Johnny with a thorny backhand.

The minuscule scratches in his cheek made Johnny laugh so hard he pissed himself and, humiliated by the dark patch in the khakis he'd started wearing in an effort to appear more sensitive, became absolutely furious.

"You . . . you . . . faggot!" Johnny Hotrod shrieked. He grabbed one horn and one fork of the trademark chin-beard (it was heavily oiled), dragged the devil to the far wall and drove his temple into the reinforced steel corner of the change machine. Again and again. It became more and more mangled but Johnny kept growling and banging until it finally shattered. Coins poured over the devil's face and showered the floor. Jackpot.

Gonna go to Vegas, gonna get me a big-titted whore, Johnny thought, eyeing a ten dollar bill stuck to the blood on the devil's forehead.

"Freeze! Right there, motherfucker!" A cop inter-rupted Johnny's plans.

Adrenaline-evil Johnny hoisted the devil over his head and stood for a moment like a crazed wrestler. The cop's partner blasted Johnny's forearm and waited for the guy in the gargoyle suit to drop onto Johnny's head. But Johnny simply shrieked in renewed fury and threw the once strongly demonic, but now sickly and broken, body at them. The two cops and the devil crashed to the floor.

"I'll suck your cock for twenty bucks."

Although there was free money all over the floor and she was dying for a hit, the prostitute was suddenly thinking in a remarkably business-like fashion. Besides, there was something special about Johnny Hotrod.

Johnny looked away from the emaciated woman, started across the carpet of money and devil blood. The obese, well-dressed man stopped him, handed him a business card. "E-mail address is on the back," he said, stepping over the devil/cop sandwich and went out the door. The student had resumed her seat in the far corner, put her Walkman on, and gone back to her textbook.

The first cop was getting up. He had his radio in his hand and he was saying "Shots fired," "Officer down," "Send help," in various numerical codes. Pleased at how calm he was. That's all he'd ever wanted to be. Cool under fire. Johnny Hotrod grabbed a fistful of blue uniform and shook him so suddenly and so violently one police boot came off and skittered down the row of dryers, bouncing off machines, stopping near the geneticist. His lips banged into the walkie-talkie and his neck snapped. Johnny stood still for a moment. He'd just killed a police officer. He turned and put the other cop out with one perfect punch.

The devil was moaning, pushing at the dead weight pinning him to the floor. Johnny grabbed the cop pistol and drilled lead into the side of the devil's head. The bullets blasted out the other side, ricocheting off the industrial tile the off-shore owners used in all their laundromats, through round dryer windows, blowing out all the lights and puncturing pipes which sprayed scalding water into the air. One of the ricochets started a fire.

Far off in the distance, sirens wailed.

"I'm one tough customer, sport," Johnny muttered to the devil who whimpered pathetically and held a hand to an ear that was no longer there. He whimpered again as he felt around, realizing there was a void behind his face.

Johnny dropped the pistol and looked for the other cop's gun. He found a fat home-rolled number tucked into the thick leather belt which he lit and left in the corner of his mouth: marijuana and cheap, sweet cigar tobacco. The second pistol was gone but he found a switchblade that had been taken off a twelve-year-old during a routine playground shakedown. Johnny flicked the gleaming blade open, caught a narrow reflection of his face and leered. Puffing, a wise old dragon, he jabbed it deep into the side of the devil's neck and with a twist and a tug, sliced all seven inches of the blade out the front, severing everything.

Unable to lift his lips and nose out of the growing puddle of his own wretched, ancient blood, sputtering, trying to warn his crazed killer, the devil gave up the ghost.

Johnny retrieved the empty pistol and was rummaging through the cop's Batman belt for more ammo when a being of light appeared.

"Okay, you've got the job."

"Huh. What job? Already got a fucken job," Johnny said, looking at his watch.

"What job? Why the one you just terminated of course. Who else are evil-minded assholes going to pick on?"

"God? You think you're God?" Johnny slid the clip into the automatic and released the slide, noisily chambering a round. He thought he was James Bond discrete.

The radiant being laughed a sad laugh. "God? God's on a whole other level." The being of light had caught the student's attention with a gentle caress. She stood, enamoured, and followed the beautiful, transcendent glow up to the front of the laundromat. Snow was falling on the police cars parked in a big semi-circle outside.

"All right, motherfucker." Johnny came around, extending the ugly little pistol and fired into the being of light. It, of course, was gone. Johnny only got off that one bullet, sitting tightly in the chamber, waiting to fly. It pierced the student's heart. She was shocked. "But, what did I do?" she asked, dropping to her knees, clutching her chest.

A big ETF motherfucker walked in the back door of the laundromat, cool helmet, goggles, butt plug (non-regulation of course), the whole nine. "Hiya Johnny," he said, recognizing his buddy from the old regiment. He shot-gunned Johnny good, then put one fist on his hip, resting the smoking barrel of the pumpgun on his armoured shoulder. He stood, ankle deep in water and blood, peering through the dim light that seeped in the dirty windows, looking around at the carnage. "Fucken shitload of paperwork," he said into his handset.

THE REGULARS

His last discernible words were, "Try and pick up every wait-ress who serves you."

— James Ellroy, at his father's deathbed

Craig opened the door to KOS, then took a step back into the teeth of the wind so a doubled over old-timer could inch out into the city. Craig had inched his own way through the city: from the third floor room of a Victorian he shared with a friend, down to College Street and along, blinded by the cold, depressed by the grey, deadly sidewalk, the filthy snow that had frozen into one painful mass, to meet old buds from high school.

He came into the diner and paused, unwinding the comically long scarf that had been left behind at a party two years ago, looking for Phil and Anil through fogged over glasses. He finally saw Phil smirking at him over Anil's shoulder. Anil turned and waved.

"What kept you, man?"

"Wind, brother. Wind."

The waitress brought a cup of coffee, two creamers nestled on the saucer beside it, without Craig having to ask. Phil had asked. Anil had requested "Some cream please, if it's no trouble." Anil was in love with her. This was the main reason they met at KOS and not across the street at Sneeky Dees which, Craig and Phil both agreed, was much cooler.

Craig nodded his thanks and continued wrestling his coat down onto the back of the chair. Anil watched the brown-eyed blond go. Not even watching her ass in tight, dyed purple jeans. Watching *her*. Phil looked at the menu. He always ordered the Greek omelet with extra feta.

"Phil got his pink slip," Anil said.

"Harris finally found your number, eh?" Craig asked.

"Yeah," Phil said. He was only twenty-six but he'd been a correctional officer for almost five years. "Finally got classified eight months ago. Bottom of the seniority list. Fifteen of us got it." He shrugged and went back to the menu.

"He's gonna take the package. Almost twenty grand!" Anil was salivating. Phil had won the lottery.

"Lotsa people with lots more time in got axed too, eh? Mortgage. Kids. All that shit?" Craig wondered.

"All that shit." It was on Phil's mind, but he didn't want to talk. "I'm outta that shit hole."

Anil frowned. He hadn't thought that the situation Phil had been put in could be hard for anyone. "Really?"

"I didn't think morale could go lower, especially since the strike." Phil said. "Everyone's bummed. Bummed or pissed." He shrugged. "Some of them are taking positions at other jails."

"They have the option?" Craig asked. He worked for the public library.

"Yeah. But check out this logic. Five of the six jails they can choose to go to are slated to close in the next year."

Craig snorted. Realized he hadn't touched his coffee, reached for the sugar. The waitress came back. Last week Anil had found out that her name was Rebecca. He asked about all the different specials listed in coloured grease pencil on a big board from a pillar in the middle of the wide, bland room. Phil ordered, smiling and nodding.

Craig scanned the menu. He ordered the first thing that sounded remotely pleasing. A sandwich of some kind. She asked about salad or fries. Told him the cook had finally figured out onion rings. She faced his profile, not afraid to open herself to him. Craig mumbled a question. Listened. Decided.

Anil watched the conversation: mesmerized. Phil pretended not to see this latest installment of speculative courtship, took stock of the general activity in the restaurant. She stepped away and Craig stopped her. Asked if she'd seen today's paper laying around. She pointed with the end of her pen to where he knew all the stray papers were shoved when the tables were bussed.

"So what're you gonna do?" Craig asked. "I dread the fucken answer."

"I'm gonna play golf in the Carolinas." He waited a beat for effect, "Next Friday!"

"God, you're a bourgeoisie asshole," Craig said.

"And in the spring, I'm gonna buy *another* motorcycle. That new Kawasaki I showed you in that mag." Phil laughed and high-fived Anil. Craig, with all his overtime, had been, by far, the best paid of the three. And he took care of them when it came to Guinness and single malt all night and DVD players on birthdays. It *was* nice.

"Tax man's gonna take a nice piece," Craig said after the food arrived. Anil stopped that first fry in mid-air. He still lived at home. Had finally finished his B.A. and started in on his master's. He'd never really worked. "You got to sock it away. Thirteen grand, or whatever you can, straight into the RRSP." Craig told Phil this every year. Phil tuned out once he remembered the first "R" was for retirement. "It's early yet, so your taxes could still work out okay."

For the first time ever, Phil nodded. "When I get back from the nineteenth hole —"

"Deadline's end of the month. Do it now and you'll be set."

"Aw, man."

"You'll be set. Could I have some mustard please?" Rebecca had come to make sure everything was okay.

"There's this film screening tonight," she told Craig when she brought the plastic yellow bottle. "This friend of mine's showing his film. It's a short. I'm on it — *in* it."

"You're in a movie?" Anil asked.

"Not starring or anything. It's, y'know, a fucked-up art movie. He's a Ryerson type. Anyhow." She took out a flyer. Anil grabbed it. He'd had the same girlfriend since they were all in high school. The daughter of his parents' friends. But she was already in medical school and Anil knew he wouldn't last in the company of the ambitious doctors-to-be she spent more and more time studying with. Rebecca took the next one out. Held on to it a beat too tight, too long, when Craig took it, making him finally look her in the eye. She was going to raise an eyebrow, turn the heat up, but she was surprised how scared he looked. "You can bring these guys if you like," she said, cooling back down.

Craig wanted to clear his throat before he spoke but he gambled and didn't. "Sounds good."

"Would you like to come down to the Carolinas next weekend and drink mint juleps with me and all my friends?" Phil held his arms out wide, as if he meant everyone in the place.

MENTION MY NAME

"Mars was setting, tangled in Virgo, somewhere over Lithuania: Jupiter shone glorious astern."
— Patrick O'Brian

Matt and Wanda were an item for three tumultuous years. Tumultuous because of Matt's drinking. Wanda finally left and Matt drank for five more. One morning he looked in the mirror and started crying. Cried for three days straight. It was like something out of the Bible. After the tears, he shaved, got a membership at a local gym, and bought a pound of very expensive coffee.

Now it's Christmas. Matt's done six years dry without A.A. or anyone else. Wanda tracks him down in the off chance he still has a certain set of negatives from way back. Matt has always been an ace photographer. He's had shows, sold work, been published. Back then he stored his negs and prints in an old steamer trunk . . . locked away from his sometimes destructive reach.

Sure he had the negs. He remembered the roll well and vividly described the exact print, a shot of Wanda's brother at Niagara Falls, that was kicking around vaguely in Wanda's memory. She wants to give it to her brother as a Christmas present.

Matt walks up the front walk of the big Howland Avenue home Wanda and her husband and son live in. Rings the bell. He has the prints in a manila envelope. No answer, although the house is lit up against the Winter's early evening. He tries the door on impulse.

"Hello," sticks his head in. Opens it a bit wider. "Hello?" puts one foot in Wanda's house. He's never been here before. Hasn't seen her in years.

"Back here," a voice shouts.

Matt closes the door behind him and puts the envelope on a small key/mail table. Should he go?

"Come on in. Matt, is that you?" the voice calls again. It's a guy.

"Ah, yeah," says Matt.

He shrugs off his wet duffel coat and hangs it on a hook beside a pair of miniature blue snowpants. Slipping off his galoshes he arms himself with the plain envelope and walks down the hall. "Hello," he says to Wanda's brother from the kitchen doorway. He and a small boy are sitting at the kitchen table wrapping Christmas presents.

"You do it," the boy says. He looks mystified.

"Okay, okay. Which bow do you want me to put?"

"Huh?"

"There, look at them all. Which one —"

"The purple one!"

"Well, okay. Purple is *your* favourite colour, but what's Mommy's?"

"Ahhh . . ."

"Wanda's upstairs. She said you may drop by. She's getting ready to go and meet Ron at his office Christmas party. I'm babysitting." Wanda's brother gives a flood of explanations to make up for his lack of greeting. "You may as well go on up."

"Ah," Matt points his right hand over his left shoulder, "up?"

"Yep, right up the stairs. Red. Go left. I think Mommy likes red."

Red. Imagine red being your favourite colour? Matt thinks as he retraces his steps. *This is already more complicated than I expected.* He walks upstairs, staring at the plush runner edged by the border of luxurious hardwood.

Ron's office has great Christmas parties. They have the crazed mood of Halloween parties plus an apocalyptic sexiness lubricated by an open bar and Christmas bonuses.

Wanda's sitting in front of the huge oval mirror at her antique makeup table. She was brushing her hair but she's stopped. An old clock radio with red numbers sits behind a boxy, off-white evening bag. Another one, black patent leather with gold furniture, sits on top of a jewellery case. The case is surrounded by a set of ivory combs, two stray lipsticks, a compact, and a pewter brandy flask with a matching cigarette lighter. Jazz is piping out of the radio and she's mesmerized by a dreamy but mathematically precise sax solo.

"Wanda? Hello?"

She turns and looks at the open door but, typically, doesn't call out, doesn't reveal her location.

Matt appears. "Hello Wanda."

She puts her hand on her chest, just below her throat but doesn't let it stay there, grateful she'd pulled on her dressing gown before sitting down.

Matt takes one step into her and her husband's bedroom but doesn't come any closer. He turns his wrist, showing the envelope without actually offering it to her.

"He's downstairs," Matt comments on how easily he could have accidentally mentioned the purpose of his visit.

"Do you know who this is?" She and Matt had met at a club during the Jazz Festival.

Matt takes another step closer. Cocks his head. He

recognizes it. Taps a finger tip against the photos lightly. "Lee Konitz." Wanda hasn't seen Matt in years. He never felt this calm. Ever. Booze and time have clawed lines around his eyes but they feel more like laugh lines, or at least like hard-earned sergeant stripes. His eyes are sharp. They don't leave her. She isn't sure if she can uncross her legs. Or if she should.

He tosses the envelope on the bed, like a contractor delivering a target kit to a professional assassin. "I forgot what size, so —" he waves at the envelope. She's looking, listening. "Mention my name at Akau. Akau on Queen West. They'll give you a deal on framing. Just —" Matt waves again.

"Mention your name."

Matt puts both hands in the pockets of his black cords. He's wearing a dark green cardigan and a loosely knotted burgundy tie. He had had lunch with his accountant then dropped by the lab to pick up some extra slide film for a shoot tonight. Then he came here. "That robe makes you look —"

Wanda holds up a sudden hand. The song has ended and the DJ's plodding, informative voice comes on. "Konitz with his twin, Warne Marsh, recorded in London, England on May 24, 1976. Peter Ind bass . . ."

"Do you have that album?"

"Yeah."

Matt walks over to the window, coming close enough to smell her, bathed but not perfumed. He looks into the backyard. It's full of snow. Some kind of fruit tree. "You never wanted to be rich," he says. It comes out as a question.

"It just worked out that way."

"That door go to a closet?"

"Uh-huh."

"Can I open it?"

Wanda doesn't answer. He opens it. "Walk-in," he tells her.

"You knew that," she says picking up a brush.

"What about that door?"

"Who does this robe make me look like?"

"I don't — I forget her name. Barbara Stanwyck, I think," he tells her.

"Bathroom," she says, poker-faced.

"Ensuite."

"You'd like to see what I have on underneath."

"The album's called *Warne Marsh meets Lee Konitz Again*. I've never seen it on CD I have a copy on vinyl." *You were with me in the store when I bought it.* Matt clearly remembers coming home that day. She had the liquor store bag. He went over to the stereo opened the bag and pulled out albums by Charlie Mingus, Clifford Brown, an Art Tatum record that he never ended up liking, and the Lee Konitz album they just heard.

Matt walks back to the door. "I could tape it for you."

"Uh-huh?"

"Have a good Christmas, Wanda."

"Matt."

He stops.

"Thanks for the photos."

Should he ask to see under the robe? Just get the hell out? Wanda had one of those bodies that looked good with no clothes on. Clothes, even lingerie, trashy or expensive, made her body seem boring and spiritless. But naked. Walking slowly towards you, coming back from the bathroom in the middle of the night with no music on . . . It was something he had completely forgotten. Until now.

Nowhere Fast

Lois passed by the bedroom door on her way to the washroom and noticed Gene hadn't bothered waiting. Flat on his back, mag propped open in one hand, dick in the other, neck twisted awkwardly as his eyes tried to make the connection between the two.

Lois surprised herself at how quickly she brushed her teeth. She'd had a full day doing inventory at the bookstore and wasn't feeling particularly horny. But now she didn't want to miss Gene blowing his wad. Maybe he'd eat her. The thought was somewhat relaxing.

"What the fuck are you doing?"

"What do you think?" His gasp turned Lois off. He glanced away from the cover of *Newsweek* for the barest of seconds, hand not missing a beat. "This chick is totally hot," he said, swallowing, not wanting to lose momentum now. *He was in the military hospital room now. She still wasn't that mobile. But she was willing and had the appetite of a backwoods girl.*

Lois put her hands on her hips and glowered beside the bed: vibing Gene's erection down. She was in panties and a T-shirt. Gene flopped down the mag, kept up a couple of optimistic strokes, then quit. "What? It's a fantasy. If it was *Penthouse* you wouldn't be pissed."

"It's sick for fuck's sake is what. Look at her. She looks like a twelve-year-old boy. She doesn't want to be in uniform. Get a fucking *Wonder Woman* comic."

"This chick went down blazing off all her ammo. Comrades dropping all around her. She was shot fulla holes," Gene propped himself up to deliver these impressive credentials. He turned as Lois came around the bed, lifted the duvet and got underneath.

"Media bullshit, Gene, and you know it." Lois made a show of fluffing her pillow and lying with her back to Gene. "I saw an interview with her father. She wasn't shot. She wasn't stabbed." Now she rolled, going up on one elbow, facing her boyfriend. "Did you even read the article?"

"No." He sounded so far from being turned on Lois felt kind of bad.

"Look, I know you're all excited by the war and all that but don't lose sight of reality and please don't bring that bullshit into our bedroom. Did you see the article in the *Globe* last weekend? It says how all the people in her town are dirt poor Bible thumpers. They *all* join the army. She's just another victim." Lois suddenly remembered how they had got on the subject of Jessica Lynch. "And you were jerking off to her. Only I could end up with a boyfriend who masturbates to fucking *Newsweek*."

"Come on, Lo. You gotta admit it's cool. Special Forces going in and rescuing her like that. Even if she didn't go down shooting."

"I don't know why you find war so sexy." Lois felt the endless day of books and numbers, hours at a computer screen behind the little desk that couldn't completely hide her from customer's inquiries about when the new Atwood would be out or if that stupid history of salt book was in paperback yet. She felt it all weighing on her again. She lay back down and pulled the duvet up around her shoulders.

The fighting part of the war seemed to be over, but who knows what will be next. It was supposed to be spring but the weather had gone cold again.

She could feel Gene hovering. He was too silent. Not saying anything, no rustling of a paperback, no resumption of the beat. "Go ahead," she mumbled. "Maybe the Marines have found the school where they trained Saddam look-alikes."

After several more moments she heard him ease off the bed and pad into the other room. She fell into an almost silent sleep, faintly aware of that high-pitched, almost invisible hum from the television. CNN.

The next day was Good Friday. Finally the long weekend had arrived. Drizzly and cool. Gene had a '96 Crown Vic and they finally had the chance drive somewhere other than Price Chopper. The car had been bought by the Boroviks, who drove it for three years before passing it on to their eldest, who drove it for two more before passing it on to the youngest, Ilya, Gene's buddy. Ilya had totally pimped the car up, tints, dark purple with flames down the side, a sound system that didn't take up the whole trunk but could still rumble the block. Two thousand and one: the summer of rap oldies. The golden age. Political rhymes, shit from P.E. and Cube — before he went Hollywood.

Now Gene listened to Steppenwolf, the first four Sabbath albums, and all the pre-'62 blues recordings he could get his hands on. He loved picking up Lo from work on a rainy night, a steaming Starbucks in her cup holder, then taking a slow drive through the city with that low-tech blues guitar poking him in the ribs like a promise he didn't want to keep.

The drive out to Ottawa, to Lo's folks' place for the weekend, was going to be great. The two hadn't spoken much over breakfast, certainly not about their disagreement the night before. They worked around each other, counting pairs of underwear and tossing them into black zippered duffle bags. Lois took the most perishable perishables from the fridge and tossed them into a plastic bag. "My mom won't know what to do with it, but this tofu won't last until Monday night."

Gene winced mentally at the thought of arriving home with most of Monday done. He'd been hoping they could slide out fairly early Monday morning and make it back in time for a matinee and a nice dinner before the long weekend expired. Instead: "I'm sure your Mom's got the place stocked. Probably even bought us some tofu."

"Probably President's Choice or some primo Japanese shit."

They both laughed and went out to the car together.

He tossed the bags on the back seat and went back in for a last minute addition to his CD wallet. When he came back Lois had already put on some tape she got from the library.

"It's a mystery," she said, pushing pause on the deck. Gene got behind the wheel, trying not to scowl. There was a chance he'd propose to Lo at New Year's and he knew that it was all about compromise. "It's just the right length given how much driving we have to do." She unpaused it and before Gene could open his mouth to say he wanted to check the radio for traffic conditions, he was distracted by the reader's lilting baritone: a girl in a dishevelled Catholic school girl's uniform sobbing in the detective's office.

Sure enough, about an hour after a Tim Hortons' highway stop Lois fell asleep. It was the perfect moment to slip on the Allman Brothers. But Gene had to find out if the school girl's mother's kidnapper would discover what was in the hotel stationery envelope that had fallen out of the mother's bag when she managed to escape by jumping out of a four-storey window onto the roof of a passing double-decker tour bus.

The weekend with the prospective in-laws should be pretty low key. Gene imagined he'd spend the large, ambiguous hours between meals in the basement, getting caught up on the latest DVD releases with Lo's sister, Karen. She was still in high school and worked at the Gap in some huge mall just outside the city. She spent all her money on the newest stuff. She didn't talk much. He didn't think she had that much to say but last visit he'd coaxed out a funny story about work.

A bunch of black-clad goth-kids had come into the store and started messing up displays, holding shirts up and saying "Ohhh, it's you" and making fun of the customers. It turned out the employee whose section they were in had no problem giving them a shove to help them find the door. And when that led to a pretty generous shove back, plus lots of fuck yous and watch it bitches, the captain of the lacrosse team and his psycho buddy came over from their section, where they helped men find the right size khaki and, excited at finally having a reason to have a go at the freaks, launched vigorously into some spring training. In the donnybrook that saw an entire rack of striped sweaters carry a gaggle of underweight mannequins through some plate glass, Lo's sister noticed a cute boy with headphones and a worn backpack take a seventy-five dollar jean jacket off a still undisturbed hanger, drape it over his arm and walk out the door. Their eyes met just as he turned to leave and he winked. She smiled, realizing she no longer gave a fuck and wanted to steal something too.

"Did you get some booty?" Gene asked.

"Uh–uh," she said, and turned back to the director's cut of *American Pie.*

That had been the weekend after New Year's. Lois had worked the entire holiday season in order to get four days in a row at Easter.

Lois woke up as Gene eased up to a stop sign. The car's lack of motion seemed strange to her as she looked around, confused for a moment by the absence of other cars. "Oh, we're here." She smiled. Gene nodded, happy at how happy she was. The mystery novel had just ended and he hadn't put any music on yet. "It'll be good to see Mom."

Lois knew her mother would make sure she was the first person she saw when she came through the door. For a second, as they stepped out onto the driveway, she imagined her father being the first family member she saw. That just wouldn't be right. But it wouldn't happen; her mom was good.

Frances hugged her daughter close and Lois let her take a good look. Lois had put on the blue cashmere sweater she bought with the gift certificate her parents had sent at Christmas. "You haven't had lunch yet, have you?" Frances asked.

"No mom, I think we're both pretty hungry." Lois delivered her line perfectly. Glanced at Gene who winked and smacked his lips silently.

"Good, because I've planned a late lunch for us all." Frances turned and called in the direction of the basement stairs then her husband's den. The troops assembled.

"The Americans are going to take over the world." Lo's sister had a boyfriend named Billy now. He had come up from the basement too, complete with stout silver hoops in each ear, hair that went carefully off in every direction and a little devil goatee. "They're already starting to threaten Syria. The American public is getting reacclimatized to seeing its sons and fathers in body bags. Now the government can just take all their military technology and make every country change to a government that will do what they say."

"They do have some pretty cool stuff," Gene said. "Like those Specter gun ships. Those things are devastating."

"No one can stop them conventionally. But that's just it," Lo's father, Amos said. He never had much time for anyone. If anything, he talked mostly about difficulties with his co-workers. He seemed to approve of Gene in a neutral, thoughtless way. Lo never stayed on the phone with him long if he answered. He was a constitutional lawyer so no one ever really understood what he did, or exactly what the shortcomings of his colleagues were.

He continued talking about the war. "It's the unconventional that's so scary. Look at those suicide bombers in Israel. Look at the September 11 hijackers. The Fedayeen Saddam were a wild card. What if just three or four of those guys got loose in Times Square?"

Gene was about to say something cutting about Muslims not being wild animals but the concern planted in the grooves between Amos's eyebrows shut him up. The fear.

"Mom, this tofu shepherd's pie is great," Lois said.

"You're right," Amos turned to Billy. It was as if he didn't notice the others. "The Americans have a real power lust going, but they don't understand what the backlash might be. No one does. The world is a completely, completely different place from, well, the Cold War. It's like we're in a science fiction movie. Or trapped in one of those damned Hollywood thrillers."

Frances reached an arm out and let it rest it gently on Amos's shoulder. It didn't fully register, but seeing her mom do this made Lois stop chewing.

Gene was still sizing up Billy. He was a little jealous of the rapport he had with Amos. Gene had been on the scene way longer but his interactions with Amos were still stiff and new.

"Another terrorist attack will just bring more lashing out," Billy said. "Lashing out at countries with small armies. And a further withdrawal of civil liberties at home," Billy said.

"I don't think it's as complicated, or as bad, as everyone makes it seem," Frances said. "No one doubts that fighting Hitler was a good thing. Well, now the Americans are being smart in going to fight Saddam. And September 11 is all the reason anyone needs."

"SARS might finish us all off first," Lois said before she could stop herself. She was confused. Her father and mother has switched places in terms of what she'd expect from them about the war.

"How is that sweetie? Have you been wearing a mask at work? I bought some bottles of anti-bacterial soap for you to take back." Frances looked from Lois to Gene.

"Do you know anyone who's been quarantined?" Karen asked.

"No," Lois said cuttingly, as if her little sister had asked the most asinine question in the world.

"Any new movies?" Gene ventured. "I'm bushed after

that drive and could do with crashing out on the couch."

"There's a Web site called New American Century. It's all about how good complete U.S. domination of the globe will be. Democracy and McDonalds for all. It's supposed to be some sort of education group. A think tank."

"Is it a dot edu?" Gene asked. He and Karen and Billy were talking in the basement.

The weekend had begun: Lois was off talking to her mom. Amos had gone back into his study. Gene had wondered about the study, and what was called the sewing room. The separation. He assumed it was something that happened with older generations. He and Lois lived in a one bedroom. They used headphones to get away from each other. He wondered if Amos and Frances ever got it on in each other's zones. He and Lois had done a lot with headphones on.

"Ah no. I think it's newamericancentury.org."

"Dot org. Right. I've been trying to figure out all those things. Then there's dot net. Do you know the difference?" Gene asked Billy.

"No, actually. Do you?" He turned to Karen.

"Me either." She shrugged without looking away from the enormous TV screen. "I never thought about it actually." *Aliens* was on with the volume muted.

"So what does this Web site say?" Gene asked.

"We should check it out. Where's the laptop?"

"It's in my bag. The battery's dead." Karen said.

"Well anyway. The freaky thing about it is that all these guys like Rumsfeld and Wolfowitz signed on to it before they were in power. Now they have little Georgie as a mouthpiece and the American public's fear of September 11 as carte blanche. No offense, Karen, but I think your mom would make a good American."

"Ah, she just needs to have things all nicely explained. Logical, that's how she is."

"What about all the protests?" Gene asked. He was thinking about Jessica Lynch and couldn't help getting a bit of an erection. He looked at Karen. She had a long neck and short hair. She was on the volleyball team.

"Protests shmotests," Billy waved them off.

Gene laughed.

"What about that asshole Don Cherry?" Karen said. "So many people don't think."

"You got that right." Billy took a monster-sized Coke off the floor beside the little coffee table and refilled his glass. He offered it to the others.

Karen held out an enormous, pink plastic glass and he filled it to the brim. "As soon as all these people see American soldiers actually fighting they suddenly assume we should be in there with them." Karen said. "Like if a friend of mine went out of her way to get into a fight then expected me to help her. What kind of friend is that?"

"This Cellucci guy is another loser," Gene said. He liked the feel the conversation had. Billy was a nice addition to the TV room.

"What about Cellucci?" Amos had come downstairs without anyone hearing him. He looked around at the piles of movie boxes, nail polish jars, rap magazines, and exercise equipment. Gene thought he looked a little lost.

"Oh, I was just thinking he's such a mouthpiece. Talking about how disappointed the Americans are in Canada. Not respecting the fact that we can think for ourselves." Gene's articulateness slid away from his tongue as he flashed on being this guy's son-in-law. Family. A quick glance showed that Billy was just staring placidly at futuristic marines going full auto against dripping space monsters. *If only it were that simple*, Gene thought.

"Have you ever met him?" Billy asked.

"Of course he has," Karen answered.

"Once or twice. Just polite introductions at cocktail parties." Amos was clearly unimpressed.

"Is he an asshole?" Gene blurted, trying to force rapport with a gamble into immature name calling.

Lo's dad shrugged. "I remember the service the Friday after September 11. The one here in town. A hundred thousand people in the middle of the day out to pay their respects. To show solidarity. That was fantastic. He should be more respectful. Chretien should boot that asshole out of the country."

"They killed our guys in Afghanistan," Karen said petulantly.

"Yes. But the service. All those people gathered for the dead." The old man didn't say anything more. Gene thought he'd become engrossed in the movie but looking over he followed his gaze down to the floor near the far corner. A Wu Tang Clan poster had fallen down, months, maybe years ago. Mostly hidden under a sweatshirt and a pair of worn out knee pads.

After a few more moments, Amos went back upstairs.

Karen turned from the screen and watched him go. When he was sure he was all the way up she turned back to the movie. "Hey Gene, you remember the big fight at the Gap I told you about?"

"Yeah."

She jerked a thumb at Billy and smiled at the television. "That's the guy who stole the jean jacket."

Gene spent Saturday morning with Lois and her mom, driving around looking at clothes, waiting for it to be lunch. When they got home, Karen disappeared with her boyfriend, leaving Gene to feel conspicuous in front of the TV by himself. He went back upstairs and browsed through the weekend paper. He liked Saddam's taste in art. The kind of stuff you see on fantasy novels, where a chick in a chain mail bikini has her spine twisted in such a way that the leather-fag looking dwarf with the sword has both a full view of her ass and a nice profile of her boobs.

There was a row of blond mug shots: would be TV versions of Private Lynch. He looked at all the faces, finally deciding there was something real about the real Private Lynch that was way more of a turn-on than all these plastic women. Amos emerged from his study after a two-hour conference call.

He saw Gene after he'd crossed well into the room. He stopped and seemed to think for a long moment. "Do you golf, Gene?"

Gene took an equally long moment to answer. "I've always wanted to learn. Do you play a lot? I know some people really get addicted to that game."

"I used to. Frances is actually more serious about it than me."

Gene wasn't sure what to do with this one. "The Americans are going to win, eh?" He had no idea where this came from.

"A foregone conclusion." Amos came around the end of the couch and sat down beside Gene. "It is disappointing that the Iraqi resistance hasn't been stiffer. I thought there would have been more volunteer battalions coming from other Arab nations."

"I think the Americans troops should have more shotguns. They're better for going house to house with —"

Amos and Gene exchanged perfectly blank looks.

Gene was about to offer to go make some coffee when at the last second he thought to ask: "Who do you think has been hacking the Al Jazeera Web site?"

They were still chatting when Lo came down from her mom's sewing room.

"Let's go," she said ignoring her father. "There's this place I want to show you."

"Don't be late for dinner. We're having roast chicken and saffron rice," her mother said as they went out the door.

Lois had disappeared while Gene browsed through an anthology of fetish lit. An expensive, glossy mag devoted to red latex dresses. They were in a small sex boutique, the kind of store Gene imagined would be in New York or Berlin. It wasn't scudgy, it catered to gays and lesbians as well as the het crowd. There was a bulletin board full of flyers and announcements about "sex positive this" and "sexual continuum that" near the end of the shelves of lubes and condoms. The place was run by anarchists.

Putting down the magazine he scanned the wall and found a coffee-table book-sized manual on that mythical Japanese bondage Lo's bookstore friends loved referring to at dinner parties. It had really clear, step-by-step instructions. The thought of fucking Lois while she was tied up was kind of weird, but he'd excelled at knots in Scouts and Lois kept reminding him she owed him a birthday present.

"Hey Gene. You think your Private Lynch has one of these?" Fortunately, no one else was in the store to witness Gene's fascinated horror at seeing his girlfriend coming at him from the change room sporting an eight-inch black silicon cock. The tattooed dyke who had helped Lois with all the little buckles and straps on the harness chuckled and might have winked before leaving her customers in peace.

"Holy shit," Gene was kind of glad they were staying at Lo's parents place. *She wouldn't bring that thing into her mother's house, would she?*

"Come on, buddy. Private Lynch is a trained killer. You don't think she's gonna put her high heels in the air for you now do you? Certainly not for a Canadian boy who's not in uniform."

Gene had to laugh; he'd never considered Jessica Lynch as a perv. "How, ah, how does it feel?" His gaze kept shifting from the moulded silicon to Lois's eyes. *Was she just clowning around or did she want to buy this thing?*

Lois leaned against the shelf and wrapped her hand around it's base. She had it on over fairly tight jeans. The old style bell above the door tinkled and a couple of women came in. They headed back towards the dildos and vibrators with only a passing glance at Gene and Lois: "That's the rig Glenda has. She says it's too —" the last words were lost on Gene and Lois as the door opened again. A guy came in and went straight over to the cash with a question.

Lois was starting to feel a little conspicuous. "I'll go take this off. You think about shaving Ryan's privates," Lois said.

"We might be late for dinner." Lois said in the car on the way home. She glanced at her watch and looked out the window. Blind Willie Johnson was on and Gene felt good. "What did you and my dad talk about after lunch?"

"The war mostly. He seems pretty concerned about it. He says a pair of those night vision goggles cost six grand each." Gene stopped, thinking.

"What?"

"It seems like the endless absurdity of it all has him really upset. I showed him those pictures of Saddam's art in the paper. You know, the stuff I was describing to you earlier."

"Yeah."

"He didn't know what to say. I mean, I was laughing and he laughed a little too. But he was just being polite. He couldn't stop staring at them either. We stopped talking. It was actually kind of awkward." Gene looked over for some kind of interpretation.

Lois was quiet for several seconds. "That's pretty weird." Then: "I'll have to ask mom."

"Why don't you just ask him. Ask him how he's doing?" Gene said bluntly.

"Not this time," Lois answered immediately. "Not this trip at least. Everything's going okay so far. Is *Ben Hur* on tonight? Do you know?" Lois knew Gene would take her signals and shut up. A few moments later he turned the music up a little and drove, nodding his head.

Everything had changed between Lois and her dad when she hit puberty. He stopped talking to her with quiet, indulgent affection. As she got older he never seemed to agree with any of her opinions. He wasn't the same with Karen. It's not that he was exceptionally nice to her, just a lot more patient and tolerant. As an adult, Lois had consciously drawn away from him. Giving him ties and predictable books at Christmas and birthdays. But she'd catch herself staring at his name, carefully signed on her cards under her mother's longer expression of best wishes for the merry or happy or whatever. In most families one person signed everyone's name. She knew. She'd asked all her friends.

Gene swooped up to the curb alongside Lo's parent's driveway. He left the driveway itself for ma's and pa's cars. And Billy's. Lois jumped out quickly. "Julie. Hey Julie, is that you?"

"Lois! No way. I was just wondering if you'd be around this weekend," the woman, holding a little boy's hand, said. She was out walking with a man who had a tiny baby strapped to his front. The baby was wearing a bright hat with a wide chin strap and seemed to look around a lot without focusing on anything.

"So who's this?" Lois knelt in front of the little boy. Introductions were made.

Julie was a high school friend who had stayed in the old neighbourhood. Gene found himself chatting with her husband, Paulo. Gene didn't know how he could be so relaxed, so comfortable with a baby, a miniature human being, on his body like that. *What if he tripped?*

"So you weren't quarantined, eh?" Paulo asked.

Gene quickly considered a coughing fit but the baby made him think it might not be funny. "Nope. No one I know has been."

"That's good. I mean, this is serious, but people around here, they don't want to know you've just been in Toronto. Some people think travel should be totally restricted."

"Between Toronto and Ottawa?" Gene asked, surprised.

"Between Toronto and anywhere." Paulo seemed cool. Seemed able to see how crazy that would be. He shrugged and pushed the first knuckle of his index finger into the baby's hand. Bounced it. The baby glanced at its hand. Wanted to look at it again but didn't quite know how. Gene couldn't take his eyes off the baby. It looked very dignified in a haphazard way. When he finally looked away, he noticed Lois staring at him. "We could be due for a little population adjustment. The earth knows. There's a lot of people in the world now. More than ever. History is full of big sicknesses. Lots of people die."

How could Paulo be saying this with this little baby fresh in his life? Gene looked closely at him. Dark circles laid siege to his eyes. The little boy came over and took Daddy's hand. Paulo looked down at him, smiling, giving him an exaggerated *isn't this great* look that transformed his cynicism and exhaustion.

"Amos!" the boy yelled, noticing the old man coming across the lawn towards them. He was in his slippers and was folding the paper he'd been reading as he strode across the lawn. "My friend gave me a Franklin backpack!" The boy blurted out the first piece of news that came into his mind.

"You have Franklin's backpack?"

"No! Franklin the turtle. He's on the backpack."

"You have a turtle in your backpack?"

"Nooo!"

Billy's old Honda Civic pulled into the driveway. The window was open, some pop music was playing and Karen was laughing.

"Oh good. We thought we were late for Mom's gourmet chicken and rice," Karen said as they came over to the group on the sidewalk. "Hi Julia. Hi Paulo. You guys remember Billy don't you?"

"Sure. This is your buddy from the Gap, right?" Julia

said. "Paulo makes the best chicken and rice in the world. Where'd you get that recipe, hon?"

Billy and Karen started chasing Julia's son around the front lawn. Amos was some sort of "home free" zone. Julia was fussing with the baby's hat while Paulo told her about the rice cooker he'd seen on sale somewhere.

"What's up?" Lois noticed Gene looking at her funny.

"I'll tell you later," Gene replied.

Lois nodded and looked down the street at the rows of trees and houses she'd spent years walking up and down, going to and from school. She looked around her now.

"We brought this really nice bottle of port," Lois said as her mom started clearing the dinner plates. "Maybe you guys would like to sit and have a drink after the dishes are done?"

"What's port?" Karen asked.

Amos was already on his way back to his study but stopped and looked at his wife.

"That sounds nice, dear. It'll just take a second to load up the dishwasher." Frances said.

Karen and Billy had only reappeared for dinner. They had plans to go to what Karen called a small party. Just a few people sitting around, probably watching TV "Oh, Billy," she said suddenly, "Could you run downstairs and get that copy of, ah, *Chicken Run*, please. We can't forget that." She turned back to the family.

"*Chicken Run*?" Lois piped up. "I've heard that's good. Maybe Gene and I should come."

Even Amos had to stifle a grin watching Karen squirm out of that one.

Amos, Lois, and Gene ended up on the elegant furniture in the living room, the least used room in the house.

"Not those," Amos said getting up from the easy chair as Frances came in with a tray of delicate liqueur glasses.

"These will do for port," Frances protested gently, but with immense confidence. Lois and Gene exchanged looks as Frances sat a little awkwardly beside her daughter on the couch. "This does look nice," Frances peered at the gold label on the bottle. "I love port, but I only seem to remember it at Christmas time."

"I know," Lois said happily. Gene was pleased too. It had been his idea.

"These glasses were a wedding present," Amos returned with the same tray but it now held what looked like four long stemmed wine glasses, but their size would have frustrated a thirsty wine lover.

"Are those claret glasses?" Gene thought he remembered something about the Three Musketeers drinking claret with roasted pheasant at some forest hideout.

"These, son, are port glasses." It was unclear whether Amos was convinced they were bona fide port glasses or if he was pointing out the arbitrariness of such a decision.

"A wedding present, eh?" Gene asked as Lois poured. "So how did you two meet anyhow?" Frances brightened as the memory took her back.

"I was a legal secretary. Amos was the summer student. He was brimming with confidence, the world his oyster." Frances smiled at her husband. Then she sighed. "He always had something for me to type."

Amos was looking into his glass, maybe smelling the bouquet as it blossomed up off the dark surface as he swirled. Then he looked sideways at Frances with the slyest look Gene had ever seen. It blew the "I'm-gonna-eat-you-alive" smirks Billy had been shooting Karen all day out of the water. He was stunned at the burning fury on Lois's face.

"Cheers!" Gene said a little too loudly and stood slightly so he could extend his glass to clink with everyone else's.

"You kids met at the bookstore, right?" Frances said.

Gene and Lois didn't even think to exchange a secret glance. This lie was in place with three-quarters of the people they knew. Gene and Lois had been set up by a mutual acquaintance named Q.T. They had both flirted with s&m, the real stuff. They soon found they were happier left to tinker comically with a bathrobe belt and a ping-pong paddle. Q.T., a silver-studded, black-leather master, who was known on three continents, had arranged for Gene and Lois to sit next to each other at an exclusive Halloween dinner two years earlier.

"That's right," Gene said. "I thought Lois was a real knockout and wanted to talk to her, but I couldn't think what to ask her. So I just went up and started babbling about Mordecai Richler —"

"I thought it was Morley Callaghan," Amos said.

Gene couldn't remember the last time they'd run through this story. *Morley? Mordecai?* "You know, it's getting so I can't quite remember. Time flies," he shrugged a fake shrug when he said this.

"It *was* Morley Callaghan," Lois said, jumping in, deciding a little confident authority is what the story needed. *We'll rehearse this on the way home.* "You were asking about *More Joy in Heaven.* The one with that wrestling angle." Lois was smiling, she liked that book a lot. Then it happened. She met her father's eye. And for the first time as an adult she met his glittering intelligence. But more importantly she met the real unconditional love, the forgiveness, and complete lack of judgment that dwelled behind his bifocals. All this, present in that moment, even though he'd just set her up. Caught her in a bullshit lie about Morley fucking Callaghan. She almost gasped.

Lois was catapulted to the very front of the locomotive of revulsion she felt toward her father. She saw the lack of track, the absence of rails as the engine roared forward. Nowhere fast. It was too much.

"How about a little more port, Frances?" Frances extended her glass. Gene poured. Amos held his glass out too. Lois studied the carpet.

Sunday was all about the meal. Gene, Billy, and Karen watched *Groundhog Day* and *Son of Robocop* before dinner. Afterwards, Karen washed the wine glasses by hand, while Gene repeatedly rearranged the contents of the dishwasher, trying to balance the serving utensils across the mountain of bread plates and dessert bowls he had noisily created. Billy leaned against the fridge drinking Coke. Lois sat on a stool laughing at Gene.

Monday morning was sleeping in late and a long breakfast. It was a little cooler than Sunday. Lois and her dad made omelets. They were her father's specialty. There was always an omelet breakfast when Gene and Lois were up.

"I'll do that," Lois had simply said, taking over beating the eggs. She then moved silently to grating cheese and chopping mushrooms. She looked at Amos, who had been watching the butter melt in the skillet. He looked at his daughter and nodded. Lois turned to the family, "Okay, who wants what? We've got broccoli and mushrooms, we've got a blend of crazy fresh herbs, cheddar or Swiss, red peppers, and shredded potato."

Karen made toast. Gene was on coffee duty, grinding

expensive beans into a luxurious black-brown dust.

Billy surfaced. Gene wondered if he had simply climbed out Karen's window, shimmied down the down spout, brushed off the dirt, and rang the doorbell. The conversation was light, the mood around the table was good.

"Lois, I'd like to talk to you," her father said to her as she and Gene piled bags in the front hall. Gene took his cue and carried bags out to the car. He was surprised when Lois appeared a moment later with the rest of their stuff.

"Let's go," she said.

Gene blinked, his mouth hanging open for only a second. There's no way they just had a talk; not the kind of talk that begins with *I'd like to talk to you.* He couldn't believe Lois, his warm sensible Lois, would stonewall her father — that she wouldn't take the opportunity to make peace. "Sure, I just have to say bye to everyone." Gene thought this was a wonderfully neutral and delicate way of leaving the door for conversation between Lo and her dad open. But only a tight-lipped mom was standing in the front hall when Gene stepped back inside. Karen, Billy, and Amos had all vanished.

"Goodbye Gene. Take care of my baby," Frances said and hugged Gene extra tight.

"Okay. Thanks for everything," Gene said. He paused. Shrugged mentally, deciding he just wanted to go listen to Sonny Boy Williamson, and turned to go. Lois was just coming back in.

Gene got the music set up and waited. Not that long really. He wondered if Amos had reappeared and was shouting at his first born.

Lois came out and got in the car. She slammed the door

and didn't say anything. Gene had been gearing himself up to force her to talk to her dad once and for all. It would be hard to insist, but it was for the good of the family. But when he saw her face the words didn't come. They sat for a moment. Then, the second before Lois said, "Come on, let's go," Gene hit it.

The blues. Appropriate and inappropriate. "He's sick." Lois finally said. Tears breaking over her face. She didn't wipe them. "Mom told me. He's really sick."

Lois knew how her mind and emotions worked. She knew she needed time to think about changing the emotional course she'd been on since puberty. She had no idea how to do this. Everything was changing. She wasn't ready for a big talk with her father and it had been easier to just turn her back. She was surprised how automatic it was. Then her mother told her. *Too much.* Now she put her face in her hands and sobbed.

They got in late. They'd spent over an hour sitting in the window of a fast food rest stop, staring silently at the highway. Drinking coffee. Letting night fall. Gene had suggested they pull over and sit down and talk, but once they joked about getting their coffee the right colour no words came.

At home they carried bags up the stairs. Shared a pot of mint tea. Got undressed. The long weekend waned. Everything was different. Gene opened his bag, took out his book and camera. He hadn't taken any pictures. Pulled out all the T-shirts and socks and underwear he'd worn since Friday and tossed them onto the heap behind the door. When the pile made the door stick diagonally out into the room it was time to do laundry. A few days later one of them would actually get around to it.

Lois did the same thing. Dutifully. She knew if she left it then Gene would do it for her and she didn't want their relationship complicated by such routines anymore. She couldn't get over the weekend. She pulled out the plastic bag from the Ottawa sex shop. She'd been so happy when she bought the rig. She thought she was finally bringing in a new level of kink, exploring something she'd masturbated privately to for over a year. But now her thoughts went way beyond midnight fun and a private smile at work the next morning. She sat down on the bed, still cradling the empty cup.

The war in Iraq was pretty much over. The looting and lawlessness had begun. Their own city was in the grip of a mysterious, international virus. Things would either get worse or better. "Remember the Norwalk virus from last winter?"

"The cruise ship virus? That's when everyone started carrying that alcohol gel for their hands, right?" Gene had thought it was a really cool product. He had driven Lois crazy, carrying it everywhere, offering it to her every half hour.

"Whatever became of the Norwalk virus?" She could hear something seductive in her voice and wondered where it came from. Her mind was on much more serious things.

Gene looked at his girlfriend. She was wearing a worn Ottawa Senators T-shirt he had never seen before. Probably Karen's. He knew she was just waiting, like a spider in its web, for him to come over there and start kissing her. He also knew that she knew that he knew. He held his bag upside down and shook it. Turned it over, looked into it, and it occurred to him that if Amos died there would be no father-in-law. He tried to imagine what that would be like. It would be much, much harder.

"Do you ever think about us having a baby?" Lois asked. "I mean, I know that's crazy and it would just change everything. I mean everything." *Dad would like it.* "Do you ever think about it?"

Gene looked at her in the mirror over the low dresser. His eyes drifted to the night stand drawer where the condoms and lube and Polaroids were kept before he could stop himself. "I think about a lot of things."

FAIRIES WEAR BOOTS

This couple had been fighting all day. In the kitchen. And I'm sure—I could almost feel my legs exploding when I shot up out of my chair—I stomped; my boots made a lot of fucking noise on the wide floor planks and that door automatically slams itself shut if you don't hold it and let the spring in slowly.

I couldn't even remember their names. But their fighting: voices not hearing each other, wrangling down from making perfect sense to pure mean digs, jabs, and slaps.

After being fairly quiet and easygoing all weekend my abrupt exit must have concerned Julie. I'd stalked down the length of the gravel drive, past the barn, and eventually pulled myself up on the high fence around the corral. Julie followed a couple of minutes later.

"They remind me of my fucken parents," I spat, furiously.

Julie didn't say anything. She squinted at me in the setting sun. She'd come out without a jacket and now she folded her arms in front of herself. The breeze was much cooler this evening. Fall was coming.

Earl had invited me out here for the weekend. His aunt and uncle were away from their farm for a couple of weeks and down the highway, in some big field, there was a punk rock, pre-Labour Day, excuse to get wasted thing going on.

Earl's aunt and uncle had gone to Florida. They loved winter in their big old farmhouse, with its wood stoves and cross-country ski trails out back. So much that they only went to Florida in the summer.

Earl and I had met in a comparative religion course: two dudes sitting at the back with headphones on pause. We made tapes for each other, shot a game of pool after class, smoked a joint in the alleyway behind the bookstore.

It turned out he'd invited *everyone*, including the screaming couple who hated each other, out to this farmhouse. The concert was just a sideshow. Some of us convoyed out to it and spent several hours wandering around, lighting spliffs every half-hour, checking out how the inner-city counterculture mixed with the local tractor pull dudes and babes.

Julie walked over toward the scorched mound that had been the ceremonial post-concert/full moon bonfire party site. She must have figured I'd come out here to be alone and I was trying to think of some conversational thing that would make her stay but I couldn't.

Her shadow stretched from her feet across the long grass until the tip of her head touched the bottom slat of the fence I was sitting on. I jumped down. She stopped, bent over and rummaged in a stray cooler abandoned as the sun rose this morning.

"I knew it! I've got a built in beer sensor. Last one." She had turned and was coming back, holding up the plain brown bottle. The label had been soaked clean off.

"It's warm," she conceded, letting me do the twist off honours.

It foamed up a little, so I held it away from us—then offered her the first slug. We passed it back and forth.

"Isaac, your parents fight, eh?"

"Fucking . . ." My voice trailed off and I looked down at the stand of trees beyond the pasture. I used to cry myself to sleep. "Years ago, man. They split up. I just—I don't know why those two got under my skin so much. All day, they've been fighting!"

"They bring out the worst in each other," Julie explained. She'd known a lot of these people since high school. I was a lone wolf.

I sighed and leaned back heavily on the fence. All weekend I'd just kind of carved out my own space and hung quiet. Still, I made sure everyone shared in the bottle of Jack I'd brought out. And they'd been equally generous.

The beer took the edge off. Julie let me drink more than half but I made sure she had the last sip. The wind blew her hair all across her face and she reached up and traced one finger along her hairline, flipping it all behind her head, making her brown eyes and pierced nose appear like a magic trick.

"You okay, partner?" Earl appeared.

"Hey man."

"Sorry 'bout the commotion."

I shrugged and shook my head a little and made some sort of dismissive grunting sound. "Julie helped," I said, holding up the empty beer and smiling at her.

"Right on."

Julie smiled back at her man and he gave her a kiss.

Earl pulled a nice fatty out of the breast pocket of the battered, faded jean jacket he always wore.

"Fucken-A," I said as he lit up. The smoke was pure Jamaican beach paradise. The last touches of sunshine made the white stringy explosion of Earl's frayed collar a work of art. Julie toked and exhaled a cloud the wind took and made longer than her shadow.

We all looked back at the beautiful, unmovable farm-house and Earl started humming an *old* Black Sabbath tune. I recognized it, all right, couldn't think of the name, but started nodding my head to the imaginary beat. I worked the roach. Earl came to the chorus. Julie started to sing.

Tomahawk

"Do you guys want perogies for dinner?" Glider asked.

"Perogies, yeah!" Mr. Singh was into it.

"I have onions and some sour cream left over from that coffee cake recipe." Reuben had discovered cooking and was trying to gain some momentum, trying to have at least some ingredients in his little one-bedroom apartment.

"We'll need more sour cream than what I saw in your fridge if we're *really* having perogies, man."

The little group fell silent. They were up at the north end of Christie Pits, not in the usual spot. All summer they'd spread out at the opposite end, just above the playground. That way they were close to Baskin Robbins, they could watch the comings and goings on Bloor Street as well as the kids on the swings, families camped out on blankets, the Rasta foot and head juggling the soccer ball.

The north side is quieter. And higher. They overlooked the entire city block that Christie Pits occupied, and had an unobstructed view of downtown: the C.N. Tower and a little to the left of it, the cluster of seventy- and eighty-storey bank towers.

They sat, watching. Waiting for something to happen.

"Remember in the summer when all that foot and mouth stuff was happening in the U.K., those Taliban fuckers destroyed those huge Buddha statues?" Reuben said.

Glider and Mr. Singh looked at him. Looked back at the silent skyline. "I remember that. That was an atrocity," his girlfriend replied. "They were huge and ancient and beautiful. Ancient spiritual art. You don't fuck with art man, it can't hurt you."

"What does that have to do with foot and mouth disease?" Mr. Singh asked.

"Nothing, man. Just they were both in the news at the same time. When I think of one I remember the other."

"Oh," Mr. Singh said.

"Those Taliban guys are some sick fuckers, man." Glider said. "I hope Bush fucks up their program."

"Oh, there's no doubt. They're going down."

"But who knows what's to come for those people. It's like Vietnam. War all the time," Mr. Singh said.

"Yeah, and they kicked Russia's ass, man." Reuben said. "They killed something like thirteen thousand troops, ten and fifteen at a time. Can you imagine how much hit and run that is, how many ambushes? Snipers? Boobytraps? That's all they did. No pitched battle. U.S. can't conquer that."

Glider looked at him.

"I mean, I think he can kill a lot of Taliban characters and force them underground, y'know. Out of power. But they'll be out there in that desert somewhere."

Glider sighed. "I guess they always will be."

"War all the time," Mr Singh said.

"Jihad," Reuben said.

"Y'know," Glider said, "I think I'm sort of switching sides here — but I think the world misinterprets Jihad. I mean, Muslims, too."

"Holy War?" Mr, Singh asked.

"I think it's really supposed to be an internal war. That's what I bet it really means in their Bible."

"The Koran."

"Whatever it's called. I think it's about the fight to be

a good Muslim, y'know. Don't covet your neighbour's wife."

"That's cause you got four wives. That would redefine coveting," Mr. Singh joked.

"No, no, no . . ."

"I know what you mean," Reuben said. "An internal struggle. That makes sense."

"More sense than, like, doing combat on other religions. That just smacks of, I don't know, finding an excuse to make a powerplay."

They fell silent again.

Watching the city.

"I'd have jumped," Mr. Singh said suddenly.

Reuben looked at him, then back at the city. Glider looked down into the scattered pockets of human activity in the park. It was quieter than usual. An Asian man reading the paper in running shoes and a business suit sat beside his bicycle, which was leaning against a park bench. He still had his helmet on.

A woman with frosted highlights and a loud voice and a gym bag went by on the sidewalk behind them. She was telling her friend how to make potato salad.

Reuben superimposed the fireball of the second plane's impact on First Canadian Place. From here, even, it would be mammoth.

"I read that they were coming out like paratroopers," Glider said. "They were lining up to —"

"It must have been awful up there," Mr. Singh said. "I mean, to jump to your certain death . . . It must have been certain death to stay. The heat, the smoke."

"Being right above that fire," Reuben continued. "I mean, it was melting the building." The three were breathless in the warm wind and the sun. Their energy, the three of them thinking the same thoughts, was paralyzing.

"Some of them called. I can't believe that. Called home to say I love you and goodbye." It was too much. Glider fought the mood. "Why were the phones still working?" she suddenly asked.

"Cellphones, I guess."

"The thing about that," Reuben began, "The *good* thing about that, is it shows a certain grace. Consciousness at the moment of death. Fearlessness. Those people showed everyone it is possible to die — with your priorities straight."

"I guess the hijackers did, too," Glider said. Reuben and Mr. Singh both looked at her sharply, but neither spoke.

The baseball diamond below them was empty.

Reuben thought about all the ice cream and popsicles they had consumed in this park during the furnace days of the heat emergencies. They were far away now. Farther away than July to October. They were gone.

"How do you stop that?" Mr. Singh asked. "That will, that iron resolve? An idea, a Stanley knife? You don't stop that with a cruise missile."

"Tomahawk," Glider said, pulling a clipboard full of blank pages out of her bag. She began folding, bending her torso over the page, making sure diagonal creases bisected corners perfectly. The guys could tell she was trying to free her mind. Mr. Singh watched her. Reuben looked up and watched a jumbo jet move silently through the sky.

"I'd have jumped," Mr. Singh said again. "There was that couple that held hands." He didn't finish.

"One of them killed a firefighter," Reuben said. "Landed on him."

Glider looked up from collapsing the page into a maze of diagonal and horizontal folds.

"No shit?" Mr. Singh said.

Glider laughed, then clamped a hand over her mouth. You don't laugh at something like that.

Mr. Singh looked down at the grass and chuckled. Reuben looked at him. Met Glider's eye. And the two of them broke up. They all laughed.

"And — and then — the whole building collapsed and killed all the —"

They stopped as if caught in a searchlight beyond a prison wall. A palpable chill ran through them.

"My God."

"There were three elite units," Reuben began. "I guess that means they were skyscraper specialists. They were all wiped out."

"You don't fucken wipe out firefighters," Glider said. She looked at the neatly folded plane.

Reuben thought she was about to crumple it viciously, but her hand shook slightly as she carefully trimmed the other wing.

Glider stood and fired the plane down into the pit. It flew parallel to the steep slope for a split second then shot up in an arc, flashing upside down over their heads before curving perfectly back down towards them. Glider neatly pinched it out of the air.

"Wow." A little kid going by on the sidewalk above and behind them pointed at Glider. He looked at his Dad and back at the woman with the pigtails and cowboy hat. She repeated the stunt. The dad let the kid walk over to get a closer look. Dad kept his distance but watched carefully.

Glider checked the up elevator on the plane's tail and turned to make another throw. Another family passing by the ball diamond had stopped and was watching too.

"What's that one called?" Reuben asked.

"It's actually called Tomahawk. I shit you not."

REBORN

"Don't worry about it," Jane tells me. "You weren't *that* obnoxious."

"But I *was* pretty drunk." I can tell from Jane's sigh that this final self-effacing comment is testing her interest in my apology. But she doesn't say anything so I stay quiet and we go back to our hangover coffees at the little table shoved up against one wall of her apartment kitchen. I wasn't too drunk to fuck, that's for sure. In fact, the maniacal enthusiasm of our copulating at three in the morning confirmed a real passion, leading to real satisfaction. It still connected us. Some self-deprecating part of me had to shoot us down by apologizing a thousand whining times.

"I used to go out with a guy who really drank. Seriously. He had a problem. All he did was get drunk. Didn't even own a television."

"Really?"

"I thought it was romantic, too. For years, well, three years. But, I mean, we were close. My dad hated him but my mom thought he was cute. Huh. After a while he didn't even want to fuck. All he did was drink and buy records. He never apologized. For being such a fuck up. Never tried . . ."

I glanced at Jane's face to confirm that she had completed her thought. But the look in her eyes — her gaze had drifted out the window, over the fire escape to the laneway — told me her mind had been pulled back in time.

"Maybe he —"

"He used to make me tapes. All this music. He used to read all about musicians. We even argued about that. I used to tell him all you need to know about a musician is on the album. Whatever. I threw them out when we broke up."

"The books?"

"The tapes. There might be one or two around." Jane got up and reached for the coffee pot. I watched the black liquid pour, and took stock of the thickness in my head, my lack of energy, achy insides, and ravenous hunger. Such Sweet Thunder. I remembered it now. On the spine of a cassette in a box Jane had under her bed. She'd pulled the box out looking for a map of N.Y.C. soon after we started dating exclusively, when the idea of going to the Big Apple came up. It had a look to it, that tape. It wasn't just a tape. It was a document, an artifact. It must be one of his.

The following Friday I arrived for our date on schedule but Jane was running a bit late. She let me in, then jumped in the shower. I got the tape out of the box under the bed and shoved it in the very bottom of my bag. Forgot about it until the middle of the following week. I was on the subway with my Walkman.

Side A was labelled "Duke" and side B "Shogun," but that was it. No song titles, no dates, no nothing. The Shogun side didn't grab me at all, could've been any afternoon show on the radio. But the Duke side totally blew me away. It started low-fi scratchy, what I figured was Duke Ellington's earliest recording. But by the end, there was everything! Wailing horns being backed fast and slow by a band so tight it was otherworldly. Evocative trios. A solo number, Duke plunking away at the keyboard, sounding never quite certain of what he was doing even though he was pure genius. Tunes and sounds I never associated with Duke Ellington filled the tape. I had to know more. I had to have more.

I got off the subway and then got back on, going in the direction of the mammoth downtown record stores. Tape still in my Walkman. I always went into the jazz section and wandered around with my one or two pop CDs in hand: slightly off-beat artists with good videos who I felt deserved to have good sales. Lost. I marvelled at the aficionados who'd take several minutes to read the back of one CD then suddenly cross to another bin, another artist and begin cross-checking. Deciphering. Regulars leaning against the counter talking jazz or just listening to the "Now Playing" CD I never knew what to buy or what to ask. So far, I had three Miles Davis albums and one Billie Holiday which didn't really do anything for me. Whenever I asked friends if they were into jazz they always had one of the same three Miles discs.

But now I walked right up to the Duke Ellington section. It was monumental. The tape was unlabelled. I got overwhelmed by the selection and the price. The cheap "Best ofs" looked too cheesy. There were too many well-priced albums labelled "Classic," and then the imports. I finally went up and interrupted the jazz experts. I asked questions. I left the store with a forty-five dollar guide book to jazz on CD I got home and took it out of the bag. The Duke Ellington section was twenty-one pages long. I browsed and read, read and scanned. I started making up a shopping list but stopped when I'd jotted down ten Duke albums that were all "essential."

"Okay, so you know what we need, or do you want to

take the list? I don't need it," Jane said. We were on a corner in Kensington Market.

"No, you go ahead and grab the bread. I'll get the veggies and meet you at the cheese store," I said.

"Don't forget —"

"Jane? Hey Jane!" This guy in a ratty cardigan and an old Canadiens toque came up to us.

"Oh. Randy. Hello." Jane was instantly uncomfortable, like she wanted to run away.

"How have you been?" Randy asked. He sounded worried about Jane, like she hadn't been doing so good the last time he saw her.

"Oh fine, just fine. Randy this is Jasper. Jas, Randy."

"Hi."

"Hey man."

"This — ah, this is the guy who used to make me all the tapes." Jane said awkwardly.

I fought back the urge to clap one hand on each of his shoulders and begin the Duke interrogation. "Oh. Uh-huh." I tried to act like I couldn't recall that conversation — Jane didn't know her pilfered tape had been on my headphones for over a week.

"Okay, so it was nice running into you Randy. I'll see you at the bakery, right?" Jane said to me and dashed off around the corner.

Randy looked after her, still concerned. There was something he wanted to tell her. But when he turned back to me his face was pleasant, gentle.

"Look. You made this tape for Jane. I don't know when. It's a mixed Duke Ellington side," I blurted.

He stopped my ramble with his eyes. I must have seemed crazy. I was Jane's new boyfriend.

"Such Sweet Thunder," he said.

"Yes!" I didn't know exactly what to ask next. I looked carefully at the corner Jane had hurried around. My lingering with her ex — this conversation must be a betrayal of some sort . . .

"It's just a sixty, right? A thirty-minute side?"

"Yes!" I said again. "But you didn't write down the songs."

"Oh," Randy said, laughing. He put his head back, he found this so funny.

"If only I had the tape with me, Randy, you could take it, listen to it —"

"I have the songs written down."

"You do?"

"I make a lot of tapes for friends so I keep a sort of log so I don't tape the same shit twice."

Wow, I thought. "That's a lot of tapes."

"Give me your number and I'll call you with the breakdown."

He didn't write my number down. Just said it back to me, leaning forward, looking intently into my face then repeating my name three times. I felt like he was blessing me. It was weird.

But he didn't call. All he had to do was jot it down, or let me jot; I'm sure he'd forgotten. But then, one day, on the answering machine, there it was. The usual message from Jane, she was coming over for our seven month anniversary dinner, then the customary beep, a deep breath and a steady recitation of song titles, album titles, and dates. The machine didn't even cut him off. He filled the little tape, neatly putting in liner-note type comments about certain solos or the difficulty of choosing one particular track off an entirely wonderful album.

There it was.

Jane arrived with a bottle of Australian Shiraz. I was making a Mediterranean hot pot for our dinner, my sister's recipe. I actually had my head in the oven, trying to read the thermometer, when the phone rang.

"Could you get that, please?" I called.

"Sure." I remember the neat clink of her wine glass being set back on the kitchen counter.

"Hello. Yeah, sure. Hang on a — Randy? Is that you?"

I closed the oven door more loudly than I'd intended then fumbled the oven mitts off, dropping them both in the process.

"Uh-huh," Jane said. She held the receiver away from her mouth. "He says for you not to buy any of the Duke records, that he can loan them to you." She went back to listening. "Really?" Jane said with so much sincere interest I felt both at ease and alone, but happy in knowing I was finally getting the inside track on *jazz*. "This Sunday, at five, at O.I.S.E.? And there'll be a sign at the elevator? Okay, well, I think I'm free so, yeah, maybe I'll see you there." She hung up. She gave me the funniest look. All the posing between us, all the cutsie affection and second guessing ourselves so as not to hurt each other fell away. Finally it was just us. "Randy's in A.A. This Sunday's his one year anniversary. His first re-birth day he called it."

"Wow, that's great," I said.

"That's great," Jane said very quietly, going deep inside for a second. Then she picked up her wine and looked from the oven to me. "So," she said brightly, openly — and I knew at that moment she would give me anything, as much as I wanted. Because on Sunday, she was going to see Randy reborn.

ACKNOWLEDGEMENTS

One Love to:
Dexter! Hannah (Visors down!) and Lovely Gretchen
(thanks for the title), Sai Ram. The Sankey Family, wel-
come Lisa and Mason. Jack David, Michael Holmes, and
all at ECW: Thank you. Black Widow Writer's Ink.
Bickford Posse, especially that tumultuous class in the
library. Ontario Arts Council. Celtic Frost, James
Baldwin, Black Flag, Cornelius Ryan, and all the others
who've blazed my trail. And finally, full metal greetings to
the T-Punch Legions Worldwide, see you crazy bastards on
tour this fall! Or e-mail: titaniumpunch@hotmail.com.